THE CHARIOTEER
OF DELPHI

THE ROMAN MYSTERIES
by Caroline Lawrence

—— A Roman Mystery ——

THE CHARIOTEER
OF DELPHI

Caroline Lawrence

Orion
Children's Books

First published in Great Britain in 2006
by Orion Children's Books
a division of the Orion Publishing Group Ltd
Orion House
5 Upper St Martin's Lane
London WC2H 9EA

A catalogue record for this book is
available from the British Library

ISBN-13 978 1 84255 256 8
ISBN-10 1 84255 256 2

Typeset at The Spartan Press Ltd,
Lymington, Hants

Printed in Great Britain by
Clays Ltd, St Ives plc

www.orionbooks.co.uk

To my hard-working agent Teresa

CIRCUS MAXIMUS IN AD80

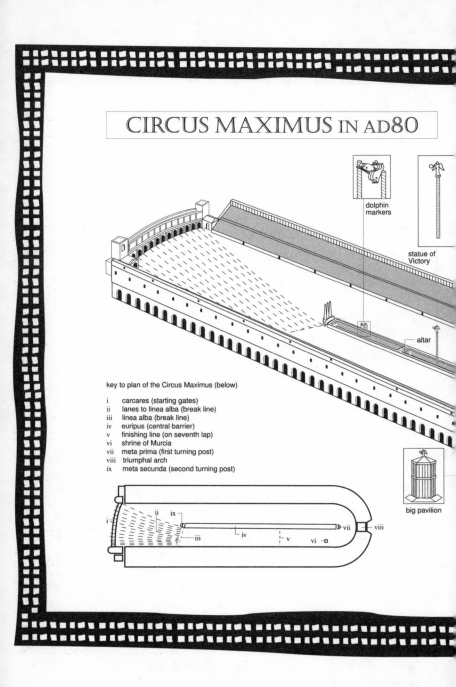

dolphin markers

statue of Victory

altar

key to plan of the Circus Maximus (below)

i   carcares (starting gates)
ii   lanes to linea alba (break line)
iii linea alba (break line)
iv   euripus (central barrier)
v   finishing line (on seventh lap)
vi   shrine of Murcia
vii meta prima (first turning post)
viii triumphal arch
ix   meta secunda (second turning post)

big pavilion

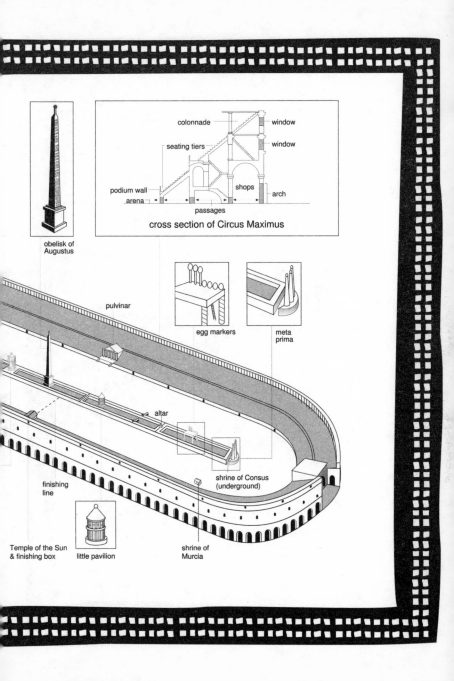

obelisk of
Augustus

colonnade — window

seating tiers — window

podium wall
arena — shops — arch

passages

cross section of Circus Maximus

pulvinar

egg markers

meta
prima

altar

shrine of Consus
(underground)

finishing
line

Temple of the Sun
& finishing box   little pavilion

shrine of
Murcia

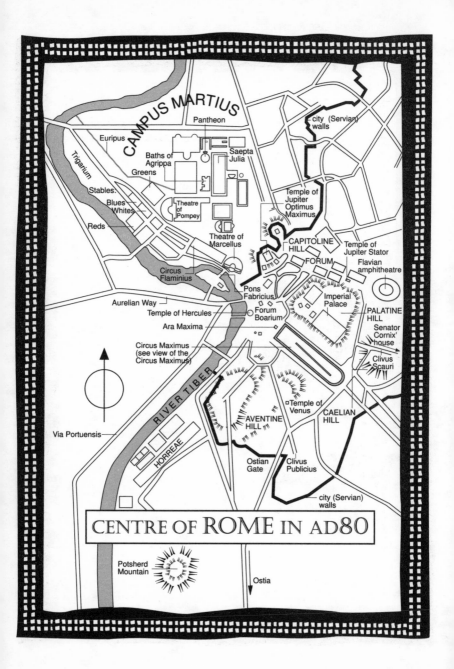

CENTRE OF ROME IN AD80

ROMAN QUADRIGA CIRCA AD80

Below: cross section of racing chariot showing detail of yoke

Bubalo (funalis) ....
Pegasus (iugalis) -----
Glaucus (iugalis) 'captain' -----
Latro (funalis) -----

bird's eye view of the Greens' alpha team showing the turning circles of each horse

This story takes place in ancient Roman times, so a few of the words may look strange.

If you don't know them, 'Aristo's Scroll' at the back of the book will tell you what they mean and how to pronounce them.

It will also explain terms for chariot racing.

The creature comes at night when the full moon is high above the desert. It has the head of a lion, the body of a goat and a snake for a tail. From its mouth comes fire, a blast of hatred that ignites all before it. Now the tents are burning and the only way past the wall of fire is to ride through it. But she is too afraid and she always wakes up screaming.

Nubia had the Blues.

She had wanted the Reds but Porcius the baker's son said nobody in their right mind supported the Reds. So she had agreed to have the Blues even though it was her birthday and she would have been perfectly entitled to her first choice.

As it was, the Reds were winning; Nubia had always been a good judge of horseflesh. Or in this case, mouseflesh. Sixteen mice pulled four tiny chariots round a twelve-foot long model of the Circus Maximus.

The model of the famous racecourse was owned by Porcius, whom Nubia and her friends had rescued from kidnappers earlier in the year. Although Porcius was only eleven years old, he was passionate about racing and knew almost everything there was to know. Two slaves from his father's bakery had carried the wooden replica of the racecourse into the sunny inner garden of the Ostian townhouse.

Nubia yawned and then smiled. After six weeks of broken nights she was tired. But today she was also happy. All her friends were here to celebrate her birthday.

'Come on, Blues!' cried the girl on Nubia's left, jumping up and down with excitement. Although Flavia Gemina was Nubia's former owner, she seemed more like a sister, even though her skin was fair and Nubia's dark.

Flavia's father, Marcus Flavius Geminus, stood beside her. Tall and clean-shaven, with the same light brown hair and grey eyes as his daughter, he wore his best summer toga as befitted the paterfamilias. On his left stood Jonathan ben Mordecai, their eleven-year-old next door neighbour. Jonathan had curly dark hair and a pleasant face. He suffered from asthma and was wheezing a little with excitement.

'Come on, Greens!' yelled Jonathan, and then cursed: 'Oh Pollux! They've stopped to investigate that leaf. Where did it come from anyway?'

'From up above!' cried Flavia. 'The gods are obviously on our side!'

Jonathan snorted with disgust, then grinned.

'Unnggh!' cried the green-eyed boy beside Jonathan. Nine-year-old Lupus had no tongue but Nubia could understand him perfectly: he was cheering for the Reds, whom he had shrewdly decided to support when Nubia went over to the Blues. Behind Lupus stood the Geminus family household slaves – the big door-slave Caudex and plump Alma, the cook. They were cheering the Whites, who had now overtaken the Greens and were coming up fast on the inside track.

'No!' wheezed Jonathan. 'Not the Whites! That means we're last!'

'Yo, Whites!' boomed Caudex, clapping his meaty hands.

'Look!' squealed Flavia. 'The Whites have taken the turn too fast!'

Nubia gasped. Sure enough, the white team's wooden chariot had overturned, and sixteen tiny pink paws scrabbled at the air.

'Naufragium! Shipwreck!' cried Porcius exultantly. And when the others stared at him he said, 'That's what you're supposed to shout when a chariot crashes.' He reached down and carefully scooped up the four writhing brown mice.

'Hey, Lupus,' said Jonathan. 'Here's a joke. How many supporters of the Reds does it take to light an oil lamp?'

Lupus shrugged, so Flavia obliged, 'Tell us, Jonathan. How many supporters of the Reds does it take to light an oil lamp?'

'Both of them!'

Everyone laughed except Nubia. 'I do not understand,' she said.

'The joke is that very few people support the Reds,' explained Flavia.

'Look!' cried Porcius. 'The Greens are running again. And they're catching up!'

Nubia's handsome young tutor Aristo bent forward to flip down the last dolphin marker in the central island of the racecourse. Nubia had chosen him to be the magistrate and referee of the race. He must have felt her gaze because he smiled up at her. Nubia quickly looked down at the three remaining chariots.

'Last lap!' shouted Captain Geminus. 'They're on the last lap!'

'Come on, Blues!' Flavia's voice cracked with excitement.

But in the end it was the Red team that took first place with the Blues second and the Greens third.

Lupus whooped and did a victory dance around the fountain. His howl of triumph was so loud that none of them heard the door-knocker.

But the dogs did. They had been shut in the store-room during the race, and their excited barks were loud enough to alert Caudex, who lumbered towards the atrium.

Lupus was still doing his victory dance around the fountain, wiggling his hips and whooping. He had plucked a leaf from a fern and was waving it like a palm branch. Presently he realised he was the only one making noise. He stopped and grinned sheepishly at them, then followed their gaze to the entryway of the garden. Standing beside Caudex was a boy in a broad-brimmed straw travelling hat and a dusty blue cloak, with a canvas bag slung over one shoulder. Nubia guessed the boy was a little older than she was: thirteen or fourteen.

'Salvete!' said the boy loudly, in Greek-accented Latin. He raised his arm in an awkward gesture of greeting. 'My name is Scopas. I come from the sanctuary of Apollo at Delphi. I seek a boy called Lupus.'

From Melissa, a novice priestess of Apollo, to her dear son Lupus.

I send this letter via Scopas, a youth from a village near

4

here. *Although I am learning to read and write, my hand is still not as steady as yours, dear son. So I am dictating this letter to Philia, who is a priestess here and my good friend. I want you to know that I am well and happy here in Apollo's great sanctuary. I trust that you and your friends are also well: this is my fervent and daily prayer to the Far-seeing One.*

I have a favour to ask of you, my dear son. I know that you live near Rome and that you know people of great influence there. Could you ask them to help this youth Scopas find a place at one of the chariot factions? The Pythia prophesied that he would be crowned in Rome. He has won the laurel wreath twice here at Delphi, though he is not yet fourteen. Please excuse his strange behaviour. A priest found him aged three, wandering in the sacred grove. His parents were never found, so the priest asked his brother to raise him. If you help Scopas, then it will help me find favour in the eyes of the priest whose brother adopted him, and also of Apollo the Far-shooter, may his name be praised.

NOW SEE! I TAKE UP THE PEN MYSELF TO WRITE IN MY OWN HAND TO SAY BE WELL, MY DEAR SON, BE WELL. AND WRITE TO ME QUICKLY!

Captain Geminus handed the letter back to Lupus. 'Thank you for letting me read the letter out loud, Lupus. And praise the gods your mother is well. We will make a thanks-offering to Apollo tomorrow.'

Lupus had been writing on his wax tablet. Now he showed it to the boy who had brought the letter: HOW IS MY MOTHER? DOES SHE LOOK WELL? IS SHE REALLY HAPPY?

Scopas stared at the wax tablet and muttered something in a strange language.

5

Lupus frowned and Jonathan said, 'Beg pardon?'

Scopas took a breath. 'Scopas cannot read,' he said, and then loudly corrected himself. 'I cannot read.'

'Lupus wants to know if his mother really is well and happy,' explained Flavia.

'I believe so.' The boy from Delphi gave a stiff nod. He was still wearing his straw travelling hat and he stood as straight as a legionary at attention. Lupus glanced at Jonathan, who raised an eyebrow at him in return.

'Well, young Scopas,' said Captain Geminus, clapping his hands and rubbing them together, 'what do we do with you now?'

'Please may he stay for Nubia's party?' Flavia asked. 'Then tomorrow we can take him up to Rome.'

'Ohe!' cried Captain Geminus. 'Whoa! Of course he may stay for the party and sleep here tonight, and I'm happy to act as Scopas's patron. But I'm afraid I don't have any connections with the racing world.'

'Sisyphus might know somebody,' said Flavia. 'He knows practically everyone in Rome.'

'Who's Sisyphus?'

'Oh, pater! I've told you myriads of times. Sisyphus is Uncle Cornix's secretary and scribe.'

'I know someone in the racing world.'

Everyone turned to look at Porcius, who continued, 'My cousin knows the head trainer of the Greens. His name is Titus Flavius Urbanus. He lost some stable boys in the big fire last winter and he's looking for new ones. You don't get paid and you have to provide your own kit and they work you like a slave, but it's your best chance of becoming an auriga.'

'What is oar rigger?' asked Nubia.

Lupus guffawed.

'An auriga,' said Porcius, 'is a charioteer. I would have applied,' he added, scuffing at the gravel pathway with his foot, 'but my father says I can't go to Rome until I'm thirteen.'

'There, pater!' cried Flavia triumphantly. 'Tomorrow we can hire a mule cart and take Scopas to Rome and introduce him to the trainer—'

'Urbanus,' said Porcius.

'—to Urbanus. It could be part of Nubia's birthday present. Nubia loves horses, don't you, Nubia?'

Nubia nodded and Lupus saw Scopas turn his whole body to face her.

'After what happened last time you went to Rome?' said Captain Geminus. 'I wonder if that would be wise.'

Lupus glanced at Flavia. He knew she hadn't told her father half of what had happened to them at the Inaugural Games in Rome.

'My father's going up to town tomorrow or the next day,' said Porcius, 'to visit his sick aunt. He could take Scopas to the Stables of the Greens. They're located in the Campus Martius.'

'Excellent!' said Captain Geminus. He turned to Porcius. 'Tell your father that if he agrees to take Scopas up to Rome, I'll pay for the mule-cart as well as the lad's kit.'

'Oh pater!' cried Flavia, 'that's so kind of you! Isn't that wonderful, Scopas? Tomorrow you'll be in Rome. Maybe even in the stables of a chariot racing faction!'

Everyone looked at Scopas, who was muttering something under his breath. Lupus was not sure, but it sounded like: 'Zip q'nee, zip q'nee, zip q'neeee!'

★

Including Scopas, there were eight people attending Nubia's twelfth birthday party that afternoon. Although Captain Geminus did not usually allow the children of his household to eat reclining, this was a special occasion. Nubia lay in the place of honour on the right of the middle couch, with Flavia and Porcius stretched out next to her. Captain Geminus occupied the host's place at the fulcrum of the couch on her right, with Aristo beside him. Jonathan, Lupus and Scopas took the couch on Nubia's left. Scopas had taken off his straw hat to reveal short dark hair, but he still wore his dusty travelling cloak, even though it was a hot afternoon.

Nubia reached up and touched her birthday present. Her friends had given her a fine gold chain for the cherrywood flute she always wore around her neck.

As Alma removed the plates of the main course, Nubia noticed that Scopas had scraped away the sauce from his stew. He had only eaten the chicken pieces and had arranged the olives and raisins in a circular pattern on his plate.

No one else noticed, for Porcius had been telling Scopas about his rescue from slave-traders in Rhodes.

'So then,' concluded Porcius, 'Lupus appears in the ship's hold with Ostia's junior magistrate and Flavia's father and a muscular man who looks like Jason, and they say, "You're all free. We're taking you home to Ostia." Isn't that amazing?'

Scopas gave a single nod. 'You have had many adventures and solved many mysteries,' he stated.

'Tell Scopas about the games at the new amphitheatre in Rome,' said Porcius. 'Nubia, tell him how you saved—'

'The games were very exciting,' interrupted Flavia, with a nervous glance at her father. 'But your life must be interesting, too, Scopas. After all, you're an auriga. Racing chariots must be very thrilling.'

'That's right,' said Aristo. 'They say it's the most dangerous job in the world!'

Scopas looked at them. 'This is correct. It is very dangerous. But Scopas is not afraid.'

Nubia studied Scopas. She had never met anyone like him. He had wide hazel eyes and a pleasant face, but it betrayed no expression. His voice was flat and loud, and his movements stiff and clumsy. Strangest of all was his occasional habit of referring to himself by name.

'How did you become a charioteer, Scopas?' asked Captain Geminus, taking a sip of wine.

'Zip q'nee,' muttered Scopas. Then he took a deep breath and spoke quickly and without inflection, as if reciting a prepared passage. 'The man who raised Scopas has a stable in Delphi village. Scopas grew up with horses. During the sacred games Scopas helped harness the horses to their chariots and drove them to the starting gates. One day an auriga became yellow so Scopas took his place.'

'Became *yellow*?' said Jonathan, raising an eyebrow. 'What does that mean?'

'Yellow. Unwell. One day an auriga became unwell, so Scopas took his place. I do not like yellow,' he added.

'And you won?' prompted Flavia, after a pause.

'Yes. I won,' said Scopas. He reached down to stroke Tigris's head and Nubia saw Jonathan raise his eyebrows in surprise. Tigris didn't usually allow strangers to touch him.

'Was it a biga or a quadriga?' asked Porcius, and

turned to Nubia. 'A biga is a two-horsed chariot and a quadriga is four.'

'It was quadriga,' said Scopas flatly.

'You don't seem very excited about racing,' said Jonathan.

'I am good at racing,' said Scopas, and added, 'Scopas does not understand people but Scopas understands horses.' He seemed to be quoting someone.

Nubia heard Lupus snicker, and she saw Flavia and Jonathan exchange a glance. Even Captain Geminus and Aristo were raising their eyebrows at each other.

Nubia caught Scopas's eye, and she gave him an encouraging smile. The others might think he was strange, but the animals liked him, and so she did, too.

SCROLL II

Two weeks later, just as Jonathan and Lupus were leaving after their morning lessons at Flavia's, a messenger appeared at the open doorway.

Jonathan tipped the man a brass sestertius and frowned down at the square of papyrus. 'It's addressed to all four of us,' he said, turning towards the girls. 'I don't recognise this seal. Or the handwriting. Hey!'

Flavia had snatched the letter from his grasp and now she eagerly thumbed off the seal. 'It's from Scopas,' she said.

'I thought he couldn't read or write,' said Jonathan.

'He can't,' said Flavia without taking her eyes from the letter. 'He dictated it to a scribe. He says he's working as a groom for the Greens and – oh!'

'What?' asked Jonathan, circling round in an attempt to see the letter.

'A prize racehorse called Sagitta has gone missing. Scopas wants us to come to Rome to try to find it.'

'Why us?' said Jonathan.

Flavia rolled her eyes. 'Because he remembered we're good at solving mysteries, I suppose.' She turned her attention back to the letter. 'Great Juno's peacock,' she breathed. 'He says the reward is a hundred thousand sesterces!'

'Nnnngh!' grunted Lupus, and pointed at the last line of the letter.

'I knew it was too good to be true,' said Jonathan, reading over Lupus's shoulder. 'The reward is only good if we find the horse before the first day of the Ludi Romani. That's four days after the Kalends,' he said, 'and today is the Kalends. Even if we arrived in Rome at dawn tomorrow that would only give us three days. It's impossible.'

'Don't be pessimist,' said Nubia, with a little smile.

'Quite right, Nubia!' Flavia turned to Jonathan. 'I say we try! We could stay with Uncle Aulus and Sisyphus could help us investigate.'

'There's only one problem,' said Jonathan.

'Yes?'

'Your father thinks Rome is dangerous. Will he let you go?'

'Good point,' said Flavia. 'We need a plan. A very clever plan.'

'Is pater back yet, Alma?' called Flavia, as she closed the front door. 'I want to ask him something.' She and Nubia had gone to the baths and then shared the Sabbath meal at Jonathan's house. Now it was after dark.

'Come and gone,' replied Alma. She was already dressed in her sleeping tunic, with her hair tied up in a scarf. 'He and Aristo have gone to dine with Cordius. They told Caudex not to wait up. And your pater took his house key with him.'

'Oh, Pollux!' muttered Flavia. 'That means they'll be home late.'

'Don't use that word. It's not ladylike.'

'What word?' said Flavia innocently. *'Late?'* She giggled and when Nubia yawned she said, 'Come on, Nubia. Time for bed.'

'Flavia?' said Nubia half an hour later.

'Yes?' The girls were in bed but not asleep. Flavia was reading a scroll by the light of her small bronze oil-lamp and Nubia was brushing her dog Nipur.

'Do you remember Pegasus from the Villa Limona?'

Flavia looked up from her scroll and frowned. 'I don't think so. Was he one of the slaves?'

'No. Pegasus was horse that refuses to run through fire when Felix rides him.'

'The dark brown horse with the blond mane and tail?' asked Flavia.

'Yes,' said Nubia, putting down the brush. 'I dream of him almost every night.'

'Nice dreams, I hope.'

'No,' said Nubia softly. 'I always dream I am riding Pegasus through fire.'

'Oh! That's terrible! Why haven't you told me before?'

'At first the dreams were not bad,' said Nubia, 'but every night they are becoming worse.'

'Is that why you cried out in your sleep last night?'

'Did I?'

Flavia nodded. 'Poor Nubia! You should imagine you're riding the other Pegasus. The one that can fly. Listen to this—' Flavia expertly turned her wrists so that the scroll moved backwards '—Where is it? Oh! Here: *Pegasus glides above the clouds and under the stars, with the sky his earth, and wings instead of feet.* That's Ovid.'

'I thought your pater does not allow scrolls of Ovid.'

'This one's permitted,' said Flavia. 'It's called *Fasti* and it's all about sacred festivals. You'd think it would be boring, but it's not. It's wonderful. Especially that part about Pegasus, the winged horse.' Flavia closed her eyes and recited: '*Pegasus glides above the clouds and under the stars, with the sky his earth, and wings instead of feet.*'

'Are his hooves having little wings either side of feet, like the god Mercury?' asked Nubia.

'No,' said Flavia. 'He has two big wings that sprout from the tops of his forelegs. Wait. I'll show you.' She put the scroll on the table, pushed off the covers and reached out to take her coin purse from the dressing table. As she emptied the contents of the leather pouch onto her bed, her dog Scuto wagged his tail and sniffed the gleaming pile of coins.

'Here!' cried Flavia, choosing a silver denarius. 'Look at this one.'

'It has profile of Domitian,' said Nubia, taking the small coin. 'Brother of Emperor Titus.'

'No, the other side.'

'Oh!' cried Nubia, her eyes wide with delight. 'It is a horse with wings.' She showed it to Nipur.

'It's Pegasus,' said Flavia.

Nubia frowned. 'Is Domitian having a flying horse?'

'Of course not. It's only a myth.'

'Tell me.'

'It all began with Medusa.'

'The monster who is so ugly she is making people turn to stone with one look?'

'Yes. Before the gods made Medusa ugly, she was stunningly beautiful. The sea-god Neptune saw her and fell in love with her and she became pregnant. She was still pregnant when the gods made her hideous and when Perseus killed her.'

'I know this,' said Nubia. 'Perseus cuts off her head and puts it in a bag.'

'Exactly. But did you know that when he cut off her head, a tiny Pegasus sprang forth?'

'Pegasus is born of Medusa?'

'Yes. His mother was Medusa and his father was Neptune, who is the god of horses as well as god of the sea. Later, when Pegasus was fully grown, a hero named Bellerophon tamed him with a magic bridle given to him by Minerva, the goddess of Wisdom. With the help of Pegasus, Bellerophon conquered the chimera, a lion-headed monster with the body of a goat and a snake for a tail.'

'Flavia! That is the creature from my dream. With the head of a lion and the body of a goat.'

'It's called a chimera,' said Flavia. 'They breathe fire.'

Nubia gasped. 'Fire!'

'That's right. Fire.'

'No,' said Nubia, pointing to Flavia's bedside table. 'Fire!' The linen scroll-case had been pushed too close to the oil-lamp and now a pretty orange tongue of flame flickered up from it.

'Fire!' screamed Flavia, leaping to her feet. 'Pater! Alma! FIRE!' Scuto and Nipur began barking as Flavia grabbed a cushion from her bed and beat the burning scroll-case. But this only excited the thin tongue of fire, and the cushion also burst into flame. Flavia squealed and dropped the burning cushion onto her bed. 'Get out, Nubia!' she cried. 'Water! We have to get water from the impluvium!' Flavia ran out of the bedroom with the barking dogs close behind.

But Nubia remained motionless. The burning bed was between her and the doorway and she found she could not move. There was something horribly familiar about this.

The flames were taking hold, making Flavia's bed a wide torch at the end of a long tunnel, and presently the only sound she could hear was the blood roaring in her ears.

'Nubia!'

She saw Flavia in the distance, standing in the remote doorway of the bedroom with a bowl in her hands and a look of horror on her face. Flavia tossed the contents of the bowl towards the flames. The water slowly rose up and described a crystal arc and shattered onto the floor, missing the fire completely.

The flames laughed and grew brighter.

For a long moment Nubia stared through the fire at Flavia's horrified face. Her friend seemed to be getting smaller and smaller, and her skin darker. It was no longer Flavia in the distant doorway, but someone else, whom Nubia could not make out.

Then everything was darkness.

SCROLL III

'Nubia, are you all right?'

A familiar-accented voice and the comforting smell of mint tea: Nubia smiled. Jonathan's father was here; she was safe.

She opened her eyes to find herself downstairs in the torchlit triclinium, propped up by cushions. A crowd of people gazed down at her. Flavia, her eyes red and swollen; Jonathan, his tunic on inside out; Lupus, his hair tousled and spiky; Jonathan's beautiful mother Susannah, her violet eyes full of concern; and Doctor Mordecai, smiling with his heavy-lidded dark eyes and extending a ceramic beaker of steaming mint tea.

Nubia took it and drank gratefully. It was fragrant and hot and sweet. It comforted her and she smiled.

'Oh, praise Juno!' cried Flavia. 'She's smiling! She's going to be all right!'

Suddenly Nipur was up on the couch, where he was never allowed to go, and his hard paws were digging into her stomach and his hot tongue was lathering her face and she was laughing and had to hold out the beaker of tea for someone to take quickly.

A moment later two big men filled the triclinium doorway, with Caudex behind them. Their thick, slightly-charred woven mats and empty buckets

17

showed that they were vigiles, men specially appointed to prevent crime and fires. They clumped into the dining room on muddy, hobnailed boots.

'That was a close call,' said one of the vigiles to nobody in particular.

'Oh, thank you very much!' said the second to Alma. He took a steaming beaker of tea from a tray she was holding. 'It is thirsty work!'

'If we hadn't arrived when we did, this whole house would be a smouldering ruin,' said the first man. 'Lucky your bedroom is part of the town wall. It's built like . . . well, like a town wall.' He took a sip of tea, then spat on the ground. 'Pollux!' he cursed. 'This isn't spiced wine.' He took another tentative sip. 'But it's good all the same. Gaius!' he said to his companion, 'try this. It's nice and sweet.'

The two vigiles sipped their mint tea and nodded at one another. Then the first one jerked his chin towards Jonathan: 'That lad is a clever one. It was the best thing you could have done: soaking cloaks in water and throwing them on the fire. Smothers the flames, you see. Good lad!' He slapped Jonathan so hard on the back that Jonathan's eyes bulged.

Lupus laughed and then everyone else began to laugh, too. And suddenly Captain Geminus and Aristo were pushing through the crowd of people, asking if Nubia was all right. They both wore dinner garlands and expressions of such concern that Nubia had to hide her emotion by burying her face in Nipur's sleek black neck.

'Up you get, you two,' said Flavia's father the next morning, coming into the triclinium. 'I have news.'

Flavia yawned and rubbed her eyes and sat up. She and Nubia had slept downstairs on the dining couches. It was a brilliant September morning, well past dawn.

'Good morning, pater!' Flavia stretched and yawned. 'How are you?'

'Good morning, sir,' said Nubia, sitting up. 'How is bedroom?'

'I'm fine, but the bedroom is not. I'll have to get the plasterer in, and the window needs a new lattice-work screen, and some of the charred ceiling beams will have to be replaced. And I've got to find the people to do it before tomorrow, because I'm off to sea.'

Flavia stopped scratching Scuto behind the ear and looked at her father. 'You're going to sea?' she said. 'Again? You've only just returned from Sicily.'

'Flavia.' She felt the couch sink as he sat on the edge of it. 'Last night my patron Cordius expressed a desire to go to Greece. He wants to charter the *Delphina* and he wants me to take him.'

'But we've already been to Greece this year.'

'He doesn't want any children along. I'll have to leave you behind.'

Flavia opened her mouth to protest, but her father hurried on: 'I know I said I wouldn't take any more voyages this season, but he *is* my patron, and he's paying me very well. Very well, indeed. And there are several weeks left in the sailing season. I thought per-haps you could go stay with your aunt and uncle in Rome. That would give the workmen time to repair your bedroom properly.'

'Rome?' said Flavia, with a quick glance at Nubia. 'You want us to go to Rome?'

'I don't *want* you to go to Rome, but I see no other choice. If your aunt and uncle are agreeable, the boys can go too. Caudex will be overseeing the work on your room, so you can take Aristo as your bodyguard. I'm not having you wandering around unchaperoned—' here he smiled at Nubia '—especially as one of you is now of a marriageable age.'

'If you insist,' said Flavia, trying to keep the excitement out of her voice. 'It will be boring in Rome, but I suppose we can find *something* to do.'

'Good!' He kissed her forehead. 'Just promise me you'll stay out of trouble.'

'Of course we will, pater,' said Flavia, but as soon as he left the triclinium she gave Nubia a huge smile and a thumbs-up. 'Euge!' she whispered. 'We're going to Rome. Isn't it exciting, Nubia? We can find the missing horse and get the reward!'

'Flavia et al!' A young Greek in a mauve tunic stepped out from beneath the shelter of a columned porch and gazed dramatically up towards the blue sky. 'Thank you, whichever of you gods have done this!' He lifted his hands in mock worship. 'You've just saved me from an extremely dull September.'

Flavia laughed and threw her arms around his waist. Sisyphus was slave and secretary to Flavia's uncle, Senator Aulus Caecilius Cornix. The senator's townhouse was located at the foot of an aqueduct on the Clivus Scauri, a quiet residential street not far from the Circus Maximus. It was early afternoon and the cicadas were creaking steadily in the umbrella pines.

Sisyphus gave Flavia a quick squeeze, then held her

at arm's length and narrowed his kohl-rimmed eyes at her. 'Are you wearing make-up, you naughty girl?'

She blushed. 'Only a little,' she said, and then grinned. 'Not as much as you!'

'Oh, you cheeky thing!' He thrust her aside in pretend disgust, then shot her a quick grin before turning on Nubia. 'Great Juno's peacock! Look at this dusky beauty. We'll have to post extra guards to keep the suitors away from you,' he gushed.

Nubia hid a giggle behind her hands.

'Jonathan, you look very fit and muscular, and so do you, my dear!' This last was addressed to Aristo, who scowled and said something in rapid Greek.

Lupus guffawed and Flavia gasped. 'Aristo! You called Sisyphus a bad word!'

'Pollux!' said Aristo with a sheepish grin. 'You're becoming far too fluent in Greek.'

Sisyphus winked at Aristo and turned to Lupus. 'My dear boy!' he said. 'Last, but never least. How are you?'

Lupus grinned and gave Sisyphus a thumbs-up.

'Any dogs?' Sisyphus looked up and down the hot, empty street.

'No dogs,' sighed Flavia. 'Pater said they had to stay at home. Jonathan's mother is looking after them.'

'Lucky her,' said Sisyphus, and then gave Jonathan a keen look. 'How's that working out, having your mother back home, I mean?'

Jonathan shrugged and looked away.

Sisyphus winced, but as they filed past him into the atrium he turned to Flavia and grinned, 'Got any good mysteries for me to solve?'

'Of course!' said Flavia. 'A missing racehorse with a reward of a hundred thousand sesterces. *If* we find him in the next two and a half days!'

SCROLL IV

Flavia's uncle Aulus was a solidly-built man of about forty-five. He had a big nose, small brown eyes, and strong opinions. He was a conservative who strongly disapproved of gladiatorial combats, beast-fights and the theatre. However, he loved the races and was a staunch supporter of the Greens.

'Yes,' he said, as a slave draped a scarlet-bordered toga around him. 'Rome has been crawling with bounty-hunters. Sagitta, the captain of the Greens' alpha team, is missing, and there's a huge reward.'

'Captain?' said Jonathan. 'I thought a horse had gone missing.'

'Sagitta is a horse. "Captain" is what they call the right-hand yoke horse, because it's the most important position.'

'Did he run away, or did somebody abduct him?' asked Flavia.

The senator shrugged. 'The popular theory is that one of the other factions took him, in order to sabotage the races and ensure their own victory.'

'Probably the Blues,' said Aulus Junior, the senator's twelve-year-old son. He spat over a low hedge, into the garden courtyard. 'The Blues are scum.'

'But surely,' said Aristo, 'one horse can't cause the downfall of a whole faction?'

'It does if the horse is one like Sagitta,' said Senator Cornix. 'He is the power behind the Green's top team. Of course, Castor could win with a team of crippled mules. He's our only hope.'

'Who's Castor?' asked Flavia. 'Is he another yoke-horse?'

Aulus Junior snickered and his father shot him a stern look. 'Castor is probably the greatest auriga of our times,' said Senator Cornix. 'He is a skilled and fearless driver. A miliarius.'

'What is milly arias?' asked Nubia.

Aristo smiled at her. 'A miliarius is a charioteer who has won more than a thousand races. Quite a feat in such a dangerous profession.'

'Is it dangerous?' said Nubia.

'Is it *dangerous*?' Aulus barked with laughter. 'At the races last month, three charioteers were trampled to death and one had his arm ripped out at the shoulder.'

Nubia shuddered.

'They say the gods have blessed Castor with invulnerability,' came a woman's voice from the shaded peristyle. Senator Cornix's wife, Lady Cynthia, was weaving at her loom.

'Wool fluff!' said the senator. 'Nobody is invulnerable. Castor is simply a brilliant horseman.' He pushed away the slave, who was smoothing folds of the toga, and turned to Jonathan. 'So where will you start your investigation?' he said.

'Um . . .' Jonathan looked at Flavia.

'We know a stable boy of the Greens,' she said. 'We're going to see him now.'

'You mean the boys are going,' said Senator Cornix. 'Surely you girls will remain here with my wife and weave, as good Roman girls should? The slaves can set up a second loom.'

'Don't bother,' said Aristo quickly, as Flavia opened her mouth to object, 'I'll stay with the girls and give them a lesson.' He winked at Flavia.

The senator grunted, nodded, then turned and called, 'Sisyphus! Have you got my bath-set?'

'Right here, sir,' said Sisyphus. He held up a brass ring with a bronze strigil, oil-flask and tweezers attached. It clinked softly as he slipped it over his forearm.

'And your writing things?'

'Of course!' Sisyphus patted a leather shoulder-bag.

'Come along, then!'

'Yes, sir!' Sisyphus rolled his eyes at Flavia and just before he followed the senator out of the house, he mouthed the words: 'Good luck!'

'This can be our lesson for today,' said Aristo over his shoulder as he led the four friends down the steep stone-paved road from Senator Cornix's house. 'How to find the stables of the four factions in the Campus Martius.'

Turning right, they walked along the long road between the Circus Maximus and the Palatine Hill. Presently they came to the Forum Boarium – the ancient cattle market – with its temples, altars, fountains and statues. As they passed beneath an arched gate in the Servian Wall, Aristo said. 'The city of Rome has spread well outside this wall. It's only function now is to keep wheeled traffic from entering Rome during the hours of daylight.'

He consulted his papyrus map and looked up. 'There's the theatre of Marcellus on our right, so the bridge on our left – with the herms and bronze balustrade – must be the Pons Fabricius, which leads to the Tiber Island.'

A surge of unpleasant memories flooded Jonathan's head as he spotted the familiar riverside stalls with their displays of votive objects and medicines. He glanced over towards the island, with its obelisk marking the sanctuary of Aesculapius. Six months ago he had fled there from a fire he had accidentally started. A fire which had claimed twenty thousand lives.

Jonathan glanced up at the Temple of Jupiter Optimus Maximus on the Capitoline Hill and then looked quickly away. The fire had started up there, and the part of Rome they were now entering had suffered the most. Jonathan had not been back since the night he fled from a wave of fire. Now he looked around with trepidation, worried about what he might see.

The damage down here on the riverbank was not too bad, but as the street angled them away from the Tiber, Jonathan noticed that some of the apartment blocks up ahead were still undergoing repair; he could see scaffolding and hear the sound of saws and hammers. One or two buildings remained charred shells, their owners presumably dead or missing.

'That's the Circus Flaminius,' said Aristo, as they emerged into a square dominated by a long, lofty building. Like the Circus Maximus, its lower storey was pierced by a series of arched arcades. 'There's very little racing here these days,' he said, 'mainly a daily flower market, as you can see. And I believe bankers and money-changers occupy those arcades. Wait for a moment while I change some coins?' He moved to one of the arches and began to speak in Greek to the man behind the table.

Jonathan and the others looked around at the bright, sunny square.

'The flowers smell very beautiful,' said Nubia, inhaling deeply.

'The fire didn't seem to harm the Circus Flaminius,' Flavia said brightly.

'Probably because it's made of stone,' said Jonathan, and added, 'All the other buildings around here were burned.'

An old beggar came up to them, and to Jonathan's horror extended a hand burnt and twisted by fire.

'Let's get out of here,' he muttered. 'Over by Aristo.'

As he turned away from the beggar, he ran straight into a man in a toga who trod heavily on his right foot.

'Hey!' scowled Jonathan. 'Watch where you're . . .' He swallowed his rebuke as the man turned and regarded him with heavy-lidded eyes, the way a bear might examine an annoying lap-dog. He was a big man, with a sweat-glazed face and balding forehead. Jonathan muttered an apology, ducked his head and hurried away. One thing he had learned in gladiator school was how to avoid a fight he could not win.

'Wise move!' The money-changer winked at Jonathan as he handed over some coins to Aristo. 'You don't want to tangle with Antonius Acutus. He's king of the Campus Martius.'

'Is he charioteer?' asked Nubia.

'Or the head of one of the factions?' asked Flavia.

'No,' chuckled the money-lender. 'Acutus runs the biggest gambling racket in Rome.'

Nubia could smell the stables before she saw them.

After leaving the Circus Flaminius, they had followed Aristo further along a street lined by partly-repaired buildings. As they passed a gilded statue of the young Hercules, she caught a whiff of horses and hay and turned to see a big red building on her left. She heard a faint horse's whinny from inside.

'That must be the Stables of Reds,' she said to Flavia.

Lupus nodded his agreement as a four-horse chariot emerged from between the red porphyry columns of a large porch, turned and rode off on the other side of a low wall.

'And that must be the Stables of the Whites.' Jonathan pointed to the building across the street from it on his right. Although it had the usual orange-red roof tiles, it was faced with dazzling white marble.

'If these are the Stables of the Reds and Whites,' said Aristo, 'then the Blues must be just up ahead and the Greens—' he consulted his map '—the Greens should be around here, too.'

But the road soon ended at an arched gate leading to grassy fields.

'Pollux!' muttered Aristo. 'We've gone too far.'

Over a low wall to the left was a long dirt track with a line of dark, flame-shaped cypress trees beyond. Nubia thought the trees probably lined the bank of the River Tiber. To the right of the arch was a vast grassy field dotted with temples and groves. She could see some boys running a race, and – further off – some men throwing javelins.

'That must be the Campus Martius,' said Flavia, indicating the field with the exercising men.

Lupus nodded. He had been here once before, just after the fire, when he had been seeking clues to Jonathan's whereabouts.

'Yes,' said Aristo, almost to himself. 'And this whole area is called the Campus Martius after it.' He consulted his map. 'So *that* must be the Trigarium.' He pointed to the long track on their left. 'Where they exercise the horses.' As if to confirm his statement, two four-horsed chariots rumbled past, throwing up twin plumes of dust which glowed golden in the afternoon sunshine.

Aristo rubbed his jaw. 'But where is the Stables of the Greens?'

Lupus grunted and pointed behind them towards a fork in the road.

'Yes, let's try that other road,' said Flavia, 'the one leading back towards that big theatre. It's not the same theatre we just passed, is it?'

'No,' said Jonathan. 'This one is much bigger. And more badly burnt,' he added under his breath.

'That's the Theatre of Pompey,' said Aristo.

Stalls and souvenir shops lined the shoulder-high wall which separated the road from the Campus Martius beyond. Lupus ran over to one of the stalls, picked up a small red whip and cracked it. Then he pretended to be a charioteer driving a team of horses.

Flavia laughed. 'I think we're back on the right track. Look at what these stalls are selling.'

One stall displayed miniature whips, curved knives and models of chariots. Another sold woven wristbands and felt skullcaps. One lamp-shop had a special display of cheap clay oil-lamps with quadriga designs stamped on them. Most of the souvenirs were available in the colours of the four factions. Nubia noticed that green and blue were the most popular colours.

There was big building up ahead, with an unusual roof of dark-green glazed tiles. It was fronted by a rank of umbrella pines, one of which had been burnt, and Nubia saw scaffolding on the far side of the upper storey.

'Behold,' she said. 'That building has green marble arch and green roof tiles. It must be Greens.'

'Judging by those guards in green tunics standing either side of the entrance,' said Aristo, 'I suspect your theory is correct.'

'The inscription reading FACTIO PRASINA over the doorway is also a good clue,' remarked Jonathan, as twin beggar-boys with curly hair ran up and held out identical grubby hands.

'Watch your coin-purse,' Flavia hissed in Nubia's ear. 'Sometimes beggars are thieves.'

Presently the curly-haired twins abandoned them for a rich woman in a sedan-chair coming the other way, but Nubia saw two other beggars sitting near a glass-ware stall by the entrance of the Greens. One was a withered old woman and the other a bearded man with a stump where his right leg should have been.

Nubia stopped to gaze at the one-legged beggar in dismay, but Flavia hooked her arm through Nubia's and pulled her firmly towards the green marble arch.

'Sorry.' One of the guards stepped briskly forward as they reached the arch. 'No entry without one of these.' He pointed to a green linen band around his wrist. It had the word 'CVSTOS' embroidered in capital letters of black thread.

'But we have an invitation from Scopas,' protested Flavia, waving the papyrus letter.

'Scopas? Who's Scopas?'

'One of your grooms.'

'Miss,' said the guard with a glance at his companion, 'do you know how many people live and work here?'

'Um . . . twenty or thirty?'

The other guard stepped forward. 'At least two hundred.'

'Two hundred?!'

The first guard nodded. 'We've got nearly two hundred and fifty horses running in the races, so we need at least fifty grooms. Plus trainers, cartwrights, saddlers, medics, priests, hortatores, moratores, desultores and sparsores. We've got over two hundred people coming and going through this arch every day. The races start the day after tomorrow and security is tight. Now, have you got identification or not?'

'But we have urgent business with him!'

'Would your urgent business have anything to do with a certain missing horse?' said the second guard.

'Yes! How did you know that?'

The first guard took a few strides forward and cheerfully kicked the one-legged beggar out of the way.

Nubia saw that the crippled man had been blocking a painting on the whitewashed plaster wall. The crude painting showed a rearing horse: a dark chestnut stallion with four white socks and a thin white blaze on his forehead. Underneath the horse was a message in neat red letters:

VALUABLE RACEHORSE MISSING: SAGITTA
REWARD OFFERED 100,000 SESTERCES
IF FOUND BY NON. SEPT REPORT TO URBANUS

'If we can't see Scopas,' said Flavia to the guard, 'then we'd like to see Urbanus!'

Guard One gave her a crooked smile. 'You and a hundred other bounty-hunters. But you can't. He's far too busy.'

'But we need more clues,' protested Flavia. 'How do we know—'

'All you need to know,' said the guard, his smile fading, 'is right there on the wall.'

SCROLL V

'Where did Lupus go?' asked Flavia suddenly.

'If that boy runs off and breaks his neck, I'll thrash him,' growled Aristo.

'Your little friend slipped into the stables while you were talking to the guards,' chuckled a voice at their feet.

Flavia turned to see the one-legged beggar grinning up at them. His dark beard did not quite cover the puckered skin of a terrible scar on the right side of his face.

She tried not to shudder. 'Thank you,' she said politely and averted her gaze.

'Look!' said Jonathan. 'Here comes Lupus. And he's with Scopas. He *did* get in!'

'Lupus!' cried Flavia. 'Praise the gods! We thought we'd lost you! And Scopas. Salve!'

Scopas flinched as Flavia went to hug him, so she stepped quickly back. She noticed he looked paler and thinner than he had in August. And he had ugly bruises on his arms.

'Is something wrong?'

'Scopas does not like people touching,' he said in his flat voice.

'I'm sorry.'

He attempted a smile. 'Thank you for helping me get a job with the Greens.'

'Are they treating you well?' asked Aristo.

Scopas's smile faded. 'Yes,' he said. 'Urbanus is very kind to me.'

'We just heard that there are over fifty grooms here,' said Flavia.

'This is correct. There are fifty-four grooms. Here are some passes,' he added, handing each of them a green wristband. 'Urbanus says you may borrow these because you are my friends. Urbanus is very kind.'

Flavia looked down at hers. Embroidered in black thread on the green cloth was one word: SPARSOR. The others were the same.

'What's a "sparsor"?' said Flavia.

'Sparsores are boys who sprinkle horses with water during the race,' said Scopas. 'To refresh them.'

'Sprinkly boys?' said Nubia.

Jonathan grinned and Lupus gave a bark of laughter.

'Well, I may not be a sprinkly boy,' said Flavia, waving her wristband as she marched past the open-mouthed guards, 'but at least I'm in!'

Nubia and her friends followed Scopas through the green arch into the Stables of the Greens.

The first room was a large bright atrium, with a rectangular skylight above and the usual rainwater pool below. There were office cubicles all round it, with men in dark green bustling here and there, writing, dictating, counting and sealing letters. Scopas did not look right or left as he led them into a large two-storey courtyard, with stalls below and living quarters above. Half a dozen boys in sea-green looked up from polishing tackle. They sat at a wooden trellis table in the shaded peristyle, near one of the massive columns of granite that supported the upper storey.

Nubia smiled. The sweet aroma of fresh hay and horse dung filled her head and caused a flood of happiness to rise in her chest. As she and her friends followed Scopas along the shaded peristyle, the horses put curious heads over the wooden half-doors of their stalls and pricked their ears.

'These stables are so luxurious,' said Flavia. 'The stalls have gilded doors.'

'Even the flies are of the highest class,' said Jonathan drily.

'Great Juno's peacock!' exclaimed Flavia. 'Look at the frescoes in this stable. Is it for a horse?'

'Yes,' said Scopas, and recited: 'This stall belonged to Incitatus, favourite stallion of the Emperor Caligula. During that Emperor's reign, it boasted an ivory manger for barley, a golden trough for water, and also a silken couch.'

'I don't see the ivory manger or the golden trough,' said Jonathan, 'but there's the couch.'

'Did horse sleep on couch?' said Nubia.

'No,' said Scopas. 'Caligula slept on that couch in this stall.'

They all stared at him.

'Zip q'nee,' murmured Scopas and then added: 'Now the stall of Incitatus is used for sick horses. Come.' He led them along the peristyle. 'We keep our best runners here in individual stalls. There is a second courtyard beyond, with other horses stabled in groups of five. Beyond that is an exercise area, with access to the Campus Martius and a canal called the euripus. There is also a cartwright's workshop and an infirmary for injured charioteers. On the upper levels—' here he gestured stiffly '—you will find pleasant dormitories for charioteers, medics, cartwrights and stable boys, as well as their families.'

Nubia nodded, hardly hearing him. She had never seen so many superb horses in one place.

'The horses are all so shiny,' said Flavia. 'And their manes seem to float.'

'The horses are brushed and massaged every day,' said Scopas. 'Hippiatros says to stroke a horse with the hand sometimes does more good than a hearty feed.'

'Who's Hippiatros?' asked Aristo.

'The stable veterinarian and medic. He is Greek, like me.'

As they approached one stall, a beautiful grey horse turned its head towards them. Flavia stopped so abruptly that Nubia bumped into her back.

'She's beautiful,' breathed Flavia.

'He is a he, not a she,' said Scopas. 'In a stable full of ungelded stallions it would not be wise to have a mare. This is Glaucus. Urbanus says his sire was Italian and his dam was from Greece.'

Nubia stroked his bony nose and gazed into his long-lashed dark eyes. 'Glaucus is both happy and sad,' she said.

'How can he be happy and sad?' asked Flavia.

'He is happy because I put him in the captain's position for a trial run today,' said Scopas, and added, 'He is an excellent captain.'

'But he is also unhappy,' said Nubia.

'This is correct,' said Scopas. 'He misses his friend Sagitta.'

'How do you know all that, Nubia?' said Flavia. 'Can you read his mind?'

'Maybe she saw that empty stall next to him,' suggested Jonathan. 'The one with "SAGITTA" painted on the door.'

For a moment they all stared into Sagitta's empty stall, then Lupus grunted and pointed to the stall beyond. Its occupant was a big stallion with a reddish-gold coat and dark brown mane.

'You like that one, Lupus?' said Jonathan.

Lupus nodded enthusiastically.

'That is Latro,' said Scopas. 'He is from Greece. He is the outside horse. They must be fast and brave.'

Lupus grinned and pointed at himself as if to say: *Just like me!*

The bronze-coloured horse moved towards Nubia and nodded his head, so that his dark forelock fell softly over his eyes. Suddenly she felt a pang in her gut. She knew immediately what it was.

'His stomach is unhappy,' said Nubia.

Scopas gave a nod. 'This is correct. Latro has colic. Yesterday Hippiatros cleansed his nether parts and is now giving him a drench of caper-bush root mixed with vinegar. It took Hippiatros thirteen days to find the problem.'

'How did you know that, Nubia?' said Flavia. 'And what is colic, anyway?'

'Colic is severe pain in the stomach,' said Jonathan.

'I know he has colic,' said Nubia, 'because my own stomach is suddenly unhappy when I touch him. But his stomach is becoming happier,' she said to Scopas. 'He likes the vinegar and caper-bush root drench.'

'This is correct.'

'Remarkable!' said Aristo and he stared at Nubia.

'What's a drench?' asked Flavia.

'Any dose of medicine given to an animal by mouth,' said Jonathan.

'Oh,' said Flavia, moving on to the next stall. 'Look at this brown one with the white socks and the little white star on his forehead. How does he feel, Nubia?'

'He is very fine.'

'That is Bubalo,' said Scopas and recited: 'He is the left-hand funalis, the unyoked inside horse. They must be steady and fearless, because they sometimes go very close to the turning post. Some people say they are more important than the captain. Urbanus says he is strong as a wild ox,' he added.

'I like him,' said Jonathan. 'I like Bubalo.' Nubia noticed he was wheezing a little.

'Those four make the alpha team,' said Scopas. 'Bubalo, Glaucus, Sagitta and Latro. But Sagitta is missing, as you see.'

'Can't they just use one of these other horses?' asked Flavia, gesturing around her. 'How about this one with the dark brown fur and black mane?' she looked at the name on the stall: 'Punctus.'

'Punctus is fast and true. But he is too small. The alpha team consists of our four biggest horses. None of the other horses are big enough to be yoked to Glaucus. The horses on a team must have legs the same length, or their stride will not match and the rhythm will be wrong when they run.'

'So what will you do?' asked Aristo.

'Our head trainer Urbanus might use a horse that recently came to us,' said Scopas. 'He is big and he is fast. Urbanus assigned him to me because I understand him. Here he is.'

For a moment Nubia's heart stood still. The horse in the next stall was as dark as she was, but his flowing mane and tail were pale gold. He was drinking from his trough but as they came up to the gilded door of his stall, he raised his head and she saw the white blaze on his nose and his liquid black eyes.

It was Pegasus, the horse from her dreams.

SCROLL VI

Nubia stared at Pegasus, the horse she had dreamed of every night for two months. He was looking straight back at her with long-lashed black eyes and he nickered softly, as if to say hello.

'By Hercules,' said Aristo. 'He's magnificent.'

The columns of the peristyle tilted and Nubia had to grip the top of the stall door to steady herself.

Flavia gasped, 'Great Juno's peacock! It's Felix's horse, Pegasus!' She turned to Nubia. 'It's the horse you told me about!'

Nubia nodded as Flavia recited the verse from Ovid: *'He glides above the clouds and under the stars, with the sky his earth, and wings instead of feet . . .'*

In his stall, Pegasus snorted again, and took a step towards Nubia.

'How do you know this horse?' asked Scopas. 'He arrived from Neapolis last month, the same day that I came to the stables.'

'We do not know him,' said Nubia, quietly opening the stall door and stepping in, 'but we have seen him from afar. And I have dreamed him.'

'Be careful,' said Scopas. 'He is nervous with strangers.'

But Nubia and Pegasus came together like friends long separated. She stroked the velvet of his nose and smelled his sweet warm breath. As she smoothed the pale gold tresses of his mane, she felt a wave of recognition and love flowing from him to her.

'Yes, Pegasus,' she whispered in her own language. 'It is I, Nubia. The one whose dreams you have been haunting.'

Suddenly he began to tremble. An image flashed into her mind and she started back as if she had been burned.

'What is it, Nubia?' cried Flavia.

'Did he bite you?' asked Jonathan.

'No,' said Nubia. 'But when I touch him I see terrible pictures.'

'What pictures?' asked Flavia.

'I see a burning tent. And a bonfire on the beach. I think these are his memories.'

'How do you do that?' asked Jonathan.

Nubia shook her head. 'It first happens with Pegasus. I make my mind smooth like a pebble and then I see pictures. Or feel feelings. Or hear words. I never do this before I meet him,' she added.

'Do you think he fears fire because of Felix's bonfire on the beach?' asked Flavia.

'No,' said Nubia. 'This fear goes back a long time. To when he was a colt, I think.'

'Can you ask him?' said Jonathan.

'Now?'

'Yes. I want to see how you do it.'

'Me, too,' said Aristo.

Nubia stroked the white blaze on Pegasus's nose, and then closed her eyes. 'I see a burning tent. But maybe that was me. My family was killed by slave-traders. Then they burned the tents of my clan.'

'Maybe Pegasus lost his family in a fire, too,' said Flavia. 'And that's why you have a special bond with him.'

'Try again,' said Jonathan, and Lupus nodded his agreement.

This time Nubia rested her cheek against the stallion's powerful neck.

'There is someone in the tent. My mother. I want to help her but I cannot. I can hear her screaming.' Nubia began to cry.

'Is that your memory or his?'

'It must be his,' said Nubia. 'My mother dies on the road to Alexandria. Oh, poor Pegasus. You were only a colt and you wanted to save your mother, but you were unable.'

She slipped her arms around his neck and suddenly saw the bonfire again. 'He is afraid.' She turned her wet face to look at Scopas. 'He is afraid you will make him jump through fire.'

'No,' said Scopas in his Greek-accented Latin. 'We train them to race chariots. There is no fire.'

'Do you hear that, beautiful Pegasus?' whispered Nubia. 'Nobody here will ask you to jump through fire.' Immediately Pegasus stopped trembling and relaxed. He breathed softly on her collarbone. She felt another wave of love flowing from him, flooding her with warmth and joy.

'Oh Pegasus,' she whispered, so that only he could hear, 'if you were mine I would never let anyone hurt you.'

'What's going on here?' said a man's voice behind them. 'Scopas, are these your friends?'

Flavia and the others turned to see a middle-aged man of medium height wearing a tunic of the Greens. He had shoulder-length sandy hair and a large flat nose. He was holding a horse-whip made of green leather and Flavia noticed that his green wristband was made of jade, not linen.

'Salve, Urbanus,' said Scopas. 'Yes. These are the friends of whom I have spoken.'

Urbanus smiled at them. 'Then I want to thank you for bringing me the most talented young groom I've ever known. This lad understands the horses better than any man here. He'll go far.' Scopas flinched as Urbanus patted him on the shoulder. 'So why are you all here? Just visiting?'

'They are good at solving mysteries,' said Scopas. 'I sent them a letter so that they will find Sagitta.'

Urbanus raised a sandy eyebrow. Then he caught sight of Nubia, still in Pegasus's stall and stroking his neck. 'Master of the Universe!' He turned to Scopas. 'I've never seen him allow anyone but you to get that close. Does the African girl know him?'

'We saw Pegasus when we were in Surrentum,' explained Flavia.

Urbanus turned to her. 'And you are . . . ?'

'My name is Flavia Gemina, daughter of Marcus Flavius Geminus, sea captain. This is my tutor Aristo and those are my friends Jonathan and Lupus. And that is Nubia. In June we were guests at the Villa of Publius Pollius Felix,' she added.

'You know the Patron?'

'Yes,' said Flavia, lifting her chin a fraction. 'His eldest daughter Pulchra is a very close friend of ours.'

Urbanus shook his head. 'Well, next time you see him, tell him he cheated me. He said this horse was an experienced racehorse from Mauritania. But so far the creature is afraid to run.'

'This is not correct, sir,' said Scopas. 'I harnessed him this morning and he ran an excellent circuit with Bubalo, Latro and Glaucus.'

'He did? You did?' Urbanus's smile seemed almost angry to Flavia.

'I can confirm that!' piped a voice from behind them. A chinless boy with spiky black hair – presumably a stable boy – was passing with a leather bucket of water. 'Scopas hitched up Glaucus in the captain's position with Pegasus as his yoke-mate and the four of them ran beautifully. That one's raced before,' he added, nodding towards Pegasus. 'No doubt about it.'

'Glaucus in the captain's position,' murmured Urbanus. 'Why didn't I think of that? He's always had a great heart.' He looked at Scopas. 'So you made Glaucus and Pegasus iugales?'

'Yes,' said Scopas. 'Glaucus gives Pegasus courage. They are good yoke-mates.'

Urbanus nodded thoughtfully. 'Perhaps we can run that team at the Saturnalia, if we can't find Sagitta. Still,' he said, 'I wish we *could* find him. He's a brave runner, with a good heart. And I miss him.' Here he turned to Aristo. 'The opening games are the day after tomorrow. If you want to join the search, I suggest you take your pupils and start looking right away.'

'Before we go,' said Flavia to Urbanus, 'do you have

44

any idea where Sagitta could be, sir? Any sightings? Any clues?'

Urbanus shook his head. Some other grooms and stable boys had gathered around him. 'Sagitta disappeared five days ago,' said Urbanus, 'the day we arrived. We like to settle the horses a week before the races, so they can get used to their new stalls.'

'So the horses don't usually live here?' asked Jonathan. He was wheezing a little.

'Live here? On the Campus Martius? Of course not. The estate of the Greens is in Nomentum. We only come to these stables for the races. When the Ludi Romani have finished we'll all pack up and go back to our stud farms. Only the scribes and accountants stay here.'

'Do you have a theory about who might have taken Sagitta?' asked Flavia. 'Who had the motive, means and method?'

Urbanus shrugged. 'Any of the other factions would have the motive. Our alpha team is – was – unbeatable. But now, without Sagitta . . .' He glanced at Pegasus. 'It's good that he can be harnessed to the others, but it takes a team of horses weeks to learn to work together. Sometimes months.'

'But how could they have got in?' wheezed Jonathan. 'The person who took him, I mean?'

'That's a mystery. You've seen how tight our security is.'

'Lupus got in,' said Flavia.

'Who?'

Lupus grinned and waved his hand.

Urbanus frowned at him. 'The guards probably thought you were a sparsor. Besides, getting in is one thing. Getting out again – with a stallion who doesn't know you – is another matter. Unless you've got a gift like hers.' He nodded at Nubia who was coming out of Pegasus's stall. 'But not many people have.'

'What if somebody from one of the other factions did manage to get in?' asked Flavia. 'And what if they were somehow able to take Sagitta out? Have you searched their stables?'

'I haven't,' said Urbanus. 'But others have – bounty-hunters wanting the reward. If Sagitta was in one of the other stables, I'd know about it by now. And don't waste your time investigating the different stud-farms. Others have been searching there, too. People have been swarming over Rome, like ants on an anthill. If you can find Sagitta where none of them have been able to, it will be a miracle.'

'Do horses make the Jonathan wheezy?' said Nubia, as they emerged from the Stables of the Greens into the blazing sunshine of a Roman afternoon and the throbbing of cicadas.

Jonathan stopped by the glass-beaker stall in the shade of an umbrella pine and nodded. 'Maybe the horses . . . or maybe all that hay . . . and dust . . . makes my asthma . . . worse. Just need . . . a few moments . . .' He opened the small herb pouch around his neck and inhaled. Nubia caught a whiff of the ephedron that brought him relief.

'Well,' said Flavia. 'We've got one good motive for the abduction of Sagitta; without him the Greens' best team is useless. Another faction must have taken him. I think each of us should hang around the other stables. Try to infiltrate and get information.'

'What is infiltrate?' asked Nubia.

'It means to get in,' said Flavia.

'I don't think I'll be any good at infiltrating the other factions,' wheezed Jonathan. 'If I go back in one of the stables I might have a bad asthma attack.'

'And my back tooth hurts like Hades,' said Aristo, touching his jaw and then wincing. 'I've got to find a tooth-puller.'

'After we infiltrate,' said Nubia with a frown, 'how do we exfiltrate?'

Aristo shook his head. 'As your appointed body-guard,' he said, 'I forbid any infiltrating or exfiltrating.'

'But Aristo!' protested Flavia.

'Give me a denarius and I'll tell you where Sagitta is!'

They all turned and looked down at the one-legged beggar sitting against his shady patch of wall. He rattled the coins in his copper beaker and smiled hopefully up at them. Something about his wide brow and straight nose reminded Nubia of a statue of Jupiter she had once seen. It occurred to her that beneath the beard and grime and terrible scars, his features were noble.

Jonathan raised his eyebrows at the beggar. '*You* know how to find a horse worth a hundred thousand sesterces and you'll tell us for one denarius?'

'Yes!' The beggar nodded cheerfully.

Lupus barked with laughter.

'If you know where Sagitta is,' said Flavia, without looking directly at the man's scarred face, 'then why don't you find him yourself?'

The beggar gestured first towards his stump and then towards the gnarled wooden crutches leaning up against the wall beside him. 'Can't move very fast.

And what would I do with half a million sesterces? All I need is my daily bread.'

Nubia felt a surge of pity for the noble beggar. She glanced over at Aristo to see his reaction; he was exploring his tooth with his tongue.

'Just one denarius,' said the beggar. 'Please?' He looked at Nubia.

'Come on, everybody,' muttered Flavia. 'Let's go somewhere else, where we won't be overheard.'

But Nubia couldn't bear to leave the crippled man with nothing. She fumbled in her coin purse. It contained a copper brooch, half a dozen pitted dates, and one silver coin. It was the denarius with Pegasus on it that Flavia had given her. How could she give him that? But it was the only coin she had, and he needed it more than she did.

'Nubia! No!' hissed Flavia, and she mouthed the words, 'He's lying. He just wants your money.'

'But he needs it,' whispered Nubia and bent to drop the silver coin in his cup.

'Thank you, kind miss,' said the beggar, and turned intelligent dark eyes up at her. 'You'll find Sagitta at the southern end of the Aventine Hill. Look in the portico gardens by the little temple of Venus on the Clivus Publicius. The temple stands at the foot of two tall cypress trees.'

Across the street, the twin beggar boys leaped to their feet and scampered off in the direction of the theatre.

'I suggest you follow them.' The beggar gave a gap-toothed grin. 'Or they'll get to Sagitta first.'

Flavia turned to stare after the twins, then she looked

back at her friends, and for a moment Nubia saw hesitation in her wide grey eyes. But only for a moment.

'Come on!' cried Flavia. 'After them!'

SCROLL VII

'Eureka!' Flavia burst from between the columns of a shady portico into sunny formal gardens.

Startled by her cry, a big horse looked up at them. He was a reddish-brown chestnut with a thin white stripe on his forehead and four white socks. He stood in the shade of two lofty cypress trees beside a small round temple.

A panting Lupus began a silent victory dance and Nubia stared wide-eyed at the beautiful stallion, her chest rising and falling after the exertion of the chase.

'I don't believe it,' gasped Aristo, emerging from between the portico columns a few moments later.

A rope tied to an elegant Ionic column rose up from the lush grass as the horse backed away, startled by their sudden arrival.

'Impossible,' wheezed Jonathan, close behind Aristo. He had untied his herb pouch and was breathing from it. 'That was . . . too easy.'

'Easy?' said Flavia, shrilly. 'You call that easy? We almost lost sight of those curly-haired beggars half a dozen times. If it hadn't been for Lupus's sharp eyes—'

'Speaking of . . . those little beggars,' gasped Jonathan, 'where have they gone? They should have got here . . . well before us. We had to stop . . . and ask those litter-bearers . . . where the temple was.'

'It doesn't matter where they are! We've found Sagitta! At least, I think it's Sagitta. You do think it's Sagitta, don't you?' She looked round at them wide-eyed.

Lupus nodded enthusiastically. He pointed at the horse, traced a vertical line on his own forehead, then pretended to fire an imaginary bow and arrow. The horse backed further away, snorting nervously.

'Of course!' breathed Flavia. 'He's called Sagitta because the mark on his nose looks like a white arrow.'

'This horse is Sagitta,' said Nubia. 'I am certain.'

'That one-legged beggar was right,' said Flavia, and looked at Nubia with awe. 'The gods rewarded you for your compassion, Nubia. Oh, thank you, Castor and Pollux!' She ran eagerly towards the horse but he reared and snorted and pawed the grassy turf with his front leg.

Flavia took a hasty step back. 'I think you'd better do it, Nubia.'

Nubia nodded and moved forward slowly, speaking softly to the horse in her own language.

The big chestnut snorted again and backed away from her, until the rope tethering him to the column was taut as a bowstring. Nubia sensed his pain and fear, so she stopped moving. Continuing to speak words of reassurance to him, she reached into her belt-pouch and pulled out a golden-brown date.

The horse tossed his head and looked at her out of the corner of his eye. He snorted again, but more softly this time.

Nubia continued speaking to him in her own

language, calmly but firmly, showing the date on the palm of her hand. 'Nobody move,' she said in Latin.

The stallion took a tentative step towards her.

Without taking her eyes from him Nubia said, 'Someone hurts him. Can you see?'

'Where?' said Flavia in a loud whisper.

'On his forelegs. Above white socks.'

'By Hercules,' said Aristo. 'It looks as if his legs have been burnt.'

'Yes,' said Nubia quietly. 'Someone is burning hair on his legs with fire.'

'Oh, the poor thing!' gasped Flavia.

The stallion stretched his neck and took the date from Nubia's hand with soft quivering lips. Then he came even closer as she slowly brought out another.

Nubia spoke softly to the horse and fed him dates. When the dates were gone, she stroked him firmly but gently, and Flavia saw a shudder run through his whole body. Presently his trembling ceased and he allowed Nubia to lead him to the column. She untied his rope and brought him to the others.

'Sagitta,' said Nubia, 'I would like you to meet my friends Flavia, Jonathan, Lupus and Aristo. Now, let us take you back to the Stables of the Greens and your friends. They are missing you greatly.'

It was almost dusk by the time they reached the Theatre of Pompey. By now they had acquired a straggling crowd of street urchins, shop-keepers and women in togas. Nubia and the big chestnut led the rowdy procession. The stall-holders at the perimeter of the Campus Martius stopped packing up and cheered when they saw the missing racehorse. Their shouts brought men pouring out of the stables of the Blues and Whites.

As they approached the Stables of the Greens, Nubia saw Flavia glance towards the umbrella pine which had sheltered the glassware stall and the one-legged beggar. The tree was silhouetted against the fading sky and there was nobody at its base.

'Look, Nubia,' said Flavia. 'Your beggar's gone.'

'He was probably one of the gods in disguise,' wheezed Jonathan. 'Maybe Jupiter. The old lady was probably Minerva and the twins were Castor and Pollux.'

'Here comes the head-trainer Urbanus,' said Aristo behind them. 'Now we'll find out if he was serious about that reward or not.'

Urbanus had come charging out of the green-roofed building, his sandy hair swinging and his green tunic flapping. But as soon as he saw them, he stopped so abruptly that Scopas and four other stable boys bumped into him. 'I can't believe it!' he cried. 'You found him! You found Sagitta!' Then he saw the horse's fore-legs. 'But what have they done to you, old boy? Master of the Universe, they've tortured him! Burned his legs . . .'

'Hippiatros knows how to make a cooling poultice,' said Scopas. 'We must put it on his legs.'

'Yes,' said Urbanus over his shoulder. 'Find Hippiatros and have him prepare a poultice right away.' He stroked Sagitta's neck and the horse shivered but did not flinch. 'You'll have a whole day to rest before the Games, won't you, my beauty?' Urbanus kissed the horse's nose and Nubia saw tears in his eyes. 'You're back and that's all that matters. Praise the Lord.'

'And then,' said Flavia over dinner that evening, 'Urbanus took us into his tablinum and gave each of us a bag with two hundred gold coins. Twenty thousand sesterces! Each!'

'I don't believe it,' said Senator Cornix. 'May the gods be praised!'

'We could barely lift the bags,' said Flavia. 'In the end we hired an eight-man sedan-chair and walked along beside it.'

'Bags of gold ride inside,' explained Nubia.

'With the curtains firmly closed!' added Flavia, and laughed as Lupus stood up and mimicked the litter-bearers staggering under the weight.

Flavia waved her left arm, showing off a green linen wristband. 'They also gave us these passes. So we can go back to the Stables of the Greens any time we like!'

'It was too easy,' muttered Jonathan, shaking his head. 'Something not right about it all.'

'What are you going to do with all that gold?' said Aulus Junior. He wore a sour expression.

'We haven't decided yet,' said Flavia.

I OWN A SHIP wrote Lupus on his wax tablet. I MIGHT INVEST MY SHARE IN THINGS TO SELL OVERSEAS

'You own a ship?' Senator Cornix raised his eyebrows at Lupus.

'May I see your bag of gold?' said Aulus Junior to Flavia.

She lifted the bag from her lap and heaved it over to her cousin. The soft leather bag was as big as a man's head.

'Are there really two hundred pieces of gold in there?' asked Flavia's nine-year-old cousin Hyacinth.

'One hundred and ninety-nine, to be exact,' said Flavia. 'I gave the litter bearers a gold coin to share out between them.'

'Twelve and a half sesterces each,' muttered Jonathan, and shook his head. 'Far too much for half an hour's work.'

'Jonathan's right,' said Senator Cornix with a frown. 'That was overly generous of you, Flavia. We'll have a great hoard of litter-bearers camping outside the house tomorrow. You should leave financial matters to the men.' He dabbed his mouth with a napkin. 'I suggest you give the rest of your gold to your father. He'll know how to invest it. Females are incapable of managing money.'

Flavia's smile turned to a scowl and she was just about to make a sharp retort when Sisyphus came into the dining room waving a wax tablet bound with a green ribbon. 'Pleased to report no litter-bearers camping outside the house, master.' He winked at Flavia. 'And this message has just been delivered by a charming young man wearing a tunic of the Greens.'

'By Hercules!' exclaimed Senator Cornix, looking up from the tablet a moment later. 'It says that Castor and his trainer would be delighted to attend a banquet here tomorrow afternoon. But how . . . ?'

'I may not know how to manage money,' said Flavia tartly, 'but I remembered the name of your favourite charioteer. I hope it's all right that I invited him.'

'All right?' A huge smile spread across his face. 'My dear girl, it's the best news I've had all year!'

★

Jonathan couldn't sleep; something was bothering him.

It had been far too easy to find the missing racehorse.

The beggar had told them exactly where the horse would be. And for only a tiny fraction of the reward he might have claimed. The twin beggar-boys had led them there and then conveniently disappeared. The reward itself had been paid promptly and without a murmur.

In his experience, nothing ever went that smoothly.

He rolled over onto his back and stared at the dim ceiling, flickering in the light of a tiny oil-lamp. Who would steal an expensive racehorse, torture him, and then return him two days before the race? Was it a warning of some kind? Or had the abductors been frightened off unexpectedly? Was there any significance to the fact that the horse had been tethered to a temple of Venus?

He turned onto his left side and stared at the frescoes on the plaster wall of the bedroom. The panels portrayed Aeneas's escape from burning Troy. Jonathan shuddered as he thought of some of the buildings he had seen today, still charred and deserted. He remembered the tidal wave of fire and the screams of the people on that terrible night. The memories caused a wave of nausea to rise up in his stomach and he looked fixedly at the one panel with no flames, trying not to let the guilt overwhelm him.

Finally the nausea passed, leaving him cold and drained. He found he was staring at a fresco of the famous wooden horse. Trojan men were pulling it into the city, while their wives and children danced in celebration. They had no idea that the wooden horse held a deadly secret, and that this would be their last night on earth.

It suddenly occurred to Jonathan that Sagitta might be a kind of Trojan Horse. But how?

SCROLL VIII

The day before the Nones of September was the Probatio Equorum, when horses would be checked for fitness by veterinarians and given practice runs in preparation for the races of the Ludi Romani. The day dawned bright and blue, with a fresh breeze from the northeast that blew away the smoke from a hundred thousand charcoal fires.

'How can you be such a pessimist?' said Flavia to Jonathan, as they approached the entrance to the Circus Maximus. 'We've just earned twenty thousand sesterces each, we're about to witness a practice chariot race and it's the most beautiful day of the year. What's bad about that?' They had pushed their way through the clamouring litter-bearers encamped outside Senator Cornix's house, hurried down the Clivus Scauri and skirted the arcaded exterior of the great circus. Now they were approaching its main entrance.

'I just think finding that horse was too easy,' muttered Jonathan.

But Flavia wasn't listening. 'Where are you going, Aristo?' she cried. 'Urbanus told us to meet him here at the Circus Maximus. The Greens have the first two hours of the morning for practice.'

'I know,' said Aristo. 'But my tooth is killing me. I

didn't sleep at all last night. I'm going to see the tooth-puller at the Temple of Aesculapius. I shouldn't be long.'

'All right,' said Flavia. 'But remember, we're only here until the third hour. Then we have to go back to the Stables of the Greens.'

He nodded. 'If I'm not back here in time, I'll meet you there.'

A guard stood in an arch beside the starting gates, but when they showed their wristbands he waved them through.

Flavia and her friends entered the Circus Maximus and stared around the hippodrome in wonder.

Tiers of empty seats rose above them on right and left, and stretched away almost to the horizon. A massive obelisk reared up in the middle of the narrow central barrier that divided the racetrack. At the far end, near the curved end of the circus, was a tiny shrine on the edge of the track. Flavia recognised it as the shrine of the goddess Murcia, near Senator Cornix's seats.

'The racecourse is deserted,' she murmured to her-self, and called out to a man raking the sand. 'Where is everyone?'

'In their pavilions,' he called. 'Other side of the carceres in the cattle market.'

Going back out through the stone arch, Flavia saw that four cloth tents had been pitched around the Ara Maxima, the great altar to Hercules. One was white, one red, one blue and one green. The rising sun made these pavilions cast long shadows across the paving stones of the Forum Boarium.

The interior of the green pavilion was filled with grooms, stable boys and charioteers. Some of them waved as they entered. Everyone knew by now that Flavia and her friends were the ones who had found their star horse: Sagitta.

The stone pavement was strewn with hay and the vast interior of the tent was filled with a pale jade light as the rising sun shone through the green linen. Flavia saw a small shrine, some wooden stalls and a curtained area near the back of the tent.

Suddenly Scopas was standing before them. Without any greeting and in his usual flat voice he said, 'Hippiatros put a cooling poultice on Sagitta's legs and he is much better today.'

'Good,' said Flavia. 'What is this place?'

'The horses are brought here from the Campus Martius,' recited Scopas. 'This is where the charioteers wait while the horses are hitched to their chariots. Horses injured in the race are brought here before they go back to the stables. Hippiatros is the stable veterinarian and medic.' Scopas pointed at a grey-bearded man examining a roan's legs. 'He is Greek, like me. There is a shrine and a table with food and drink.' He gestured towards the curtained-off area. 'There is a latrine, too. Urbanus has another reward for you.'

'He already gave us a fortune in gold,' said Flavia. 'What else could he give us?'

'Greetings, my young friends.' Urbanus came up behind Scopas. His sandy hair hung loose around his shoulders and his dark eyes were smiling. He gestured with his green whip. 'You can see the horses are just arriving from the Campus Martius. We're going to give them a practice run around the hippodrome. Some of the horses have never been here before and this will help them get used to the course. We're going to give all twenty-four teams a gentle run, in two lots. If you like, you can each have a go.'

Scopas turned to them. 'Urbanus said I can drive, too. As I did at Delphi. I must go and get dressed.' He moved away.

Lupus grunted excitedly, mimicked holding the reins, and raised his eyebrows.

'Oh, no!' laughed Urbanus, stroking his big flat nose. 'It takes years to learn to manage a team of four stallions. Each of you four will ride behind an experienced auriga. If you want to, that is.'

'We want to!' said Flavia, her heart beating fast.

'Come on, then!' Urbanus led them out of the pavilion into the bright morning sunshine where stable boys were harnessing horses to chariots.

'Why do they bind horses' hair with green ribbons?' asked Nubia.

'Their manes have to be tied neatly so they don't get tangled in the reins,' said Urbanus, 'and the tails need to be clubbed like that so they don't fly up in the charioteer's face. Who'd like to ride in this chariot?' he said, patting the rump of a dark brown stallion. 'Cresces may be young but he's one of our best drivers.'

'Me!' Flavia waved her hand enthusiastically and then blushed. With his sparkling blue eyes and straight nose, Cresces was extremely good-looking. He wore a short grass-green tunic and fawn-coloured leggings with green leather straps around them. Around his torso was a stiff leather jerkin, of darker pine-green. She couldn't tell the colour of his hair – he wore a tight-fitting green leather cap – but she guessed from his eyebrows that it was black.

Lupus went with a team of jet-black stallions driven by an African auriga whose skin was almost as dark and gleaming as the horses'. Jonathan let Urbanus assign him to a team of dark bay horses with a roan captain and a hawk-nosed charioteer.

'You can ride with me,' said Urbanus to Nubia, tucking his long hair up into a leather helmet with visor and chin strap.

'Can't Nubia ride with Scopas?' said Flavia.

'Better not,' said Urbanus. 'He's just a tiro – a novice – and the team he's taking out is third rate.' He looked at Nubia. 'Why don't you come with me? I'm driving Sagitta's team.'

Flavia grinned as Nubia solemnly followed the head trainer towards a fountain dominated by a bronze bull. The spiky-haired groom was letting the alpha team drink from the trough. Sagitta's lower legs were bound with strips of green. He stood in the captain's position next to Glaucus, with Bubalo on the inside and Latro on the outside.

Flavia turned back to examine her own team. 'Are we going to ride in *that*?' she asked the handsome charioteer, pointing to a small construction of wicker and leather attached to the long pole of the yoke.

Cresces nodded as he stepped up into it. 'The lighter the chariot is, the faster it goes.'

'But it's hardly more than a basket on wheels!' she protested. 'Where will I stand?'

'Very close behind me! And you'd better hang on tight. Not yet,' he laughed. 'I haven't been strapped in.' Two stable boys had run forward and were wrapping the ends of eight leather reins around Cresces's stiff leather jerkin. He turned away from Flavia and concentrated on helping them get the length right. When the reins were taut, one of the grooms held out a wickedly sharp curved knife. Cresces fitted this into his leather jerkin and looked over his shoulder at Flavia. 'In case I get thrown from the chariot,' he explained, showing her his dimples. 'I can cut myself free of the reins.'

'Why don't you just hold the reins in your hands?'

'Look.' He gathered the reins in his left hand. 'See how big a handful all eight reins would make? It would be hard to hold that for a quarter of an hour. Also, we use our bodies to steer as much as we use our hands. I can make them go right—' he leaned his body to the right '—or left.' He tipped the other way. 'Also,' he said, selecting one of the reins and twitching it, 'I can make each individual horse speed up or slow down.' He accepted his green leather whip from a stable boy and flicked the horses into motion. The wooden wheels made a rattling noise as a boy helped guide the team across the paving stones of the forum towards the starting-gates. Flavia followed close behind.

There were twelve gates in all, sturdy stone arches wide enough for a four-horse team. Above the gates was a colonnaded gallery. Flavia knew the magistrate and some of the stewards watched the races from up there. She saw Nubia's team being guided into the arched gate on her right and Jonathan was already stepping up behind the hawk-nosed auriga on her left.

'Porcius would be sick with envy if he knew what we were doing,' called out Jonathan.

'I know,' agreed Flavia. 'I wish he could be here with us.'

From somewhere above came the brassy blare of

trumpets and the horses began to stamp their feet and toss their heads.

'Oh!' cried Flavia, as Cresces's chariot began to roll back towards her.

'Get up behind me! Quickly!' said Cresces over his shoulder. 'You're safer up here than down there. They blow the trumpets just like they do at the real races to get the horses used to it. What they can't reproduce is the roar made by a quarter of a million Romans when the gates fly open.'

'Great Juno's peacock!' muttered Flavia, as she stepped up behind him. 'The chariot's floor is bouncy!'

'That's because it's leather webbing on a wicker frame,' he said with a laugh. 'Makes it much easier going over the bumps. You'll have to hang on tighter,' he added, 'or you'll fall off and be trampled to a paste.'

'Juno!' gasped Flavia. 'Don't say that!' She thought about making the sign against evil but decided it might be safer to follow his advice, so she wrapped her arms tightly around his waist. She could feel the stiff bumpy leather of the reins wrapped around his pine-green jerkin, and she could smell his laurel hair oil and the faint musky smell of his underarms. The leather webbing of the floor jounced them gently as the chariot moved towards the arched stall.

'It's like being on board a ship,' Flavia muttered.

'Without the shipwreck, I hope!' joked Cresces.

The moratores stepped forward to guide the horses into the stalls. They were dressed in green for each faction had its own. Flavia knew their job was to keep the horses calm.

'Are these the carceres?' asked Flavia as they moved

into the vaulted space, dim after the brightness of the forum.

'That's right,' said Cresces, and his voice echoed in the confined space. 'They're called that because they're like prison cells. In a moment those wooden gates in front of us will fly open, and it's like being set free. Are you ready?'

'*No,*' thought Flavia, but she said, 'Yes.'

The trumpet blared again and one of the horses in front of her lifted his pretty balled tail and deposited a load of manure on the sandy floor of the stall. The pungent smell of dung and leather filled her head.

'Better out than in!' laughed Cresces but he did not turn round. Flavia could feel him trembling. The horses were excited, too, and she was intensely aware of their stampings, snorts and whinnies.

'Hang on, children!' came Urbanus's voice from the stall to her right. 'The third blast is about to come. Hang on tight!'

A moment later the trumpet uttered a sustained blare and the wooden doors of the carceres flew open. They were off!

SCROLL IX

As her chariot exploded out of the stalls, Nubia screamed and clutched Urbanus's waist beneath the coil of leather reins.

Entering the morning arena was like plunging into a pool of water. She was aware of the vast cool space above her and of a line of pounding horses stretching away to her left and right. The chariot floor was bouncing so much that at times she was airborne.

Above the thunder of nearly two hundred hooves on the sandy track, she could barely hear what Urbanus was shouting over his shoulder:

'We all have to stay in our lanes until we reach the linea alba, that white line on the track up ahead. And then—' here he tipped his body to the left '—we can try for the inside lane!' He laughed as Nubia screamed again. She had almost fallen out of the little chariot.

Now the landmarks of the central barrier were flashing by on her left: two lofty green marble columns with a row of bronze dolphins on top, an altar, a discus-thrower, a spiral pillar with a statue of a winged victory, a pavilion and the massive obelisk on its square base. To her right were tier upon tier of empty seats not yet illuminated by the sun.

Urbanus's whole body moved as he drove, leaning first one way, then the other, even bending forward at the waist to urge on the horses. Nubia closed her eyes for half a circuit and held tight to his lean torso in its stiff leather strapping, but the bouncing of the wicker and leather chariot made her feel sick so she opened her eyes again, just in time to see the cones of the meta prima rushing up on her left. They were like three enormous bronze cypress trees planted very close together.

'Hang on,' bellowed Urbanus, 'and have a look behind to see how far ahead we are!' Leaning in, he gave a deft tug of the innermost rein with his left hand. Nubia gasped as they took the turn. They were so close to the meta that she could see the intricate designs carved into the nearest cone and she could feel a breeze caused by their passage. For a sickening moment the chariot skidded sideways in a spray of sand. After a protesting squeal the wheels began to turn again as the horses regained the straight. The chariot's speed increased.

Nubia had forgotten to look around but through the monuments on the barrier she caught a flash of black horses and a black-skinned driver. Lupus's team must be close behind. She could see the rest thundering behind them.

Soon they were coming up to another meta – the turning point closest to the carceres from which they had first emerged. This time Nubia knew to lean into the turn as Urbanus took the chariot in a tight skidding arc. Then the wheels bit sand and then they were bouncing down the straight again. Above the sound of their own horses' hooves Nubia heard another drumming thunder and saw something out of the corner of her eye. A dark shape, two, three, four nodding horses' heads as a team of bays began to overtake them on the right.

Nubia looked over and saw that Scopas was driving.

He was leaning so far forward at the waist that his body was horizontal and he seemed to float. Every iota of his being was focused on his horses and on the track ahead.

Nubia gasped as Scopas's chariot hit a bump and he rose up into the air. But he came down as nimbly as an acrobat, his concentration never faltering. He might be stiff and awkward on land, but behind a team of four stallions Scopas was as lithe as a dancer. She saw his left hand give a subtle twist on the two inside reins while at the same moment he touched the tip of his whip to the captain's rump. The bay team effortlessly overtook them, moved into the inside lane and – like a dancer's ribbon – flowed smoothly around the meta out of sight.

Urbanus and Nubia were left breathing Scopas's dust.

Scopas easily won the practice circuit, followed by a red-headed Gaul named Eutychus and then Lupus's team of blacks. As the African's team crossed the finishing line ahead of him, Jonathan saw Lupus hanging onto the charioteer's belt with both hands, leaning back and whooping in terrified joy.

The finishing line was opposite the steward's box a little more than halfway down the right-hand side of the course. Jonathan knew the horses needed a full half length to slow down after their final burst of speed. The charioteers rounded the meta and allowed their foaming horses to slow down for the final half circuit. Before passing through the arch to the right of the carceres, his chariot came to a halt. A boy ran up and prised Jonathan's fingers free from Hawk-nose's leather jerkin and helped him down from the chariot.

Jonathan's legs were trembling so violently that he was only able to stagger a few steps out of the way before he collapsed onto the track. Laughing hysterically, he crawled over to Flavia, who was also sitting in the cool sand. Nubia came up a few moments later, her golden eyes dazed. She sat down beside them.

Two young sparsores ran up with jugs of water in wicker casings. Jonathan's laughter had turned to hiccups which made it hard to drink.

'Dear gods!' he gasped, once he had enough moisture in his mouth to speak. 'I have never been so terrified in my entire life.'

'I know,' said Flavia, and passed the water jug to Nubia with shaking hands. 'Pollux! I have a piece of grit in my eye.'

'Don't rub it,' said Jonathan, 'or you could scratch your eye. Hold your nose and blow gently. That should dislodge it.'

'That's better,' said Flavia. 'It's gone. Ugh! There's sand in my mouth, too. Dear Juno! What an experience!'

Lupus came dancing up to them, waving a tiny palm branch and wiggling his hips.

'You didn't win, Lupus,' protested Jonathan.

Lupus put up three fingers.

'You are coming three?' said Nubia.

Lupus nodded.

'Who came first?' asked Flavia. 'I had my eyes closed the whole time.'

Lupus made his face expressionless and stood with his arms pressed to his sides, like an archaic statue.

'Scopas?' said Flavia with a giggle.

Lupus nodded.

'Stiff as a pillar,' said Jonathan, and hiccupped.

'He is not stiff when he drives,' said Nubia, handing the wicker-covered water jug back to one of the sparsores. 'He drives like Apollo.'

'Really?' said Flavia.

Nubia nodded.

'Where did you get the victory palm, Lupus?' hiccupped Jonathan.

Lupus gestured vaguely in the direction of the barrier which ran down the centre of the race track.

'Well done for coming third, Lupus,' said Flavia. 'Now stop showing off and collapse in a heap like the rest of us.'

But Lupus wasn't listening. He had let his jaw drop in mock astonishment and was staring at the carceres. The three friends turned their heads to follow his gaze.

'What are you staring at?' said Flavia. 'Those statues between each of the starting gates? They're called herms. I know you've seen ones like them before, Lupus. They're everywhere.'

Lupus pointed and giggled.

'I've told you a dozen times, Lupus,' said Flavia patiently. 'They're not rude, they're prophylactic. They turn away evil.'

Lupus grinned and sat beside Jonathan, who was now hiccupping resignedly.

'You four all right?' Urbanus came up to them, his

whip in one hand and a glass beaker in the other. He had taken off his leather helmet and although his long sandy hair was dark with sweat, his eyes were sparkling. He took a sip from his beaker. 'Wasn't that fun?'

'Fun?' croaked Jonathan. 'My life passed before me like a scroll unrolling.'

'Why did we go so fast?' asked Flavia. 'I thought it was supposed to be a slow practice circuit.'

'You think that was fast?' laughed Urbanus. 'Didn't you notice? We barely used our whips. And I was actively holding my lot back. We don't want to exhaust them before tomorrow's race.'

'You were holding back?' gasped Flavia.

Urbanus laughed again. 'Of course! In a real race the horses go twice as fast. And they do it for over double that length. We only completed three circuits today; they'll run seven tomorrow. Over two miles.'

'Amazing,' said Flavia.

'Overweening,' murmured Nubia.

'Unbelievable,' hiccupped Jonathan, and then exclaimed, 'That must be why Scopas won!'

'Oh, no,' said Urbanus with a chuckle. 'Believe it or not, he was holding back, too, though I've never seen that team run so well . . .'

Jonathan hiccupped again and Urbanus extended his glass. 'Drink some posca. Never fails to cure hiccups.'

Jonathan took the beaker. It was mould-blown glass, pale blue-green with little raised chariots running around it. He drank. 'Aaargh!' he choked. 'It's almost pure vinegar!'

'But your hiccups are gone, aren't they?' asked Urbanus. Somewhere a trumpet blared.

Jonathan waited a moment, then nodded.

'Then up you get.' Urbanus grinned and took back the beaker. 'Our second lot of chariots will be out of the gates in a few moments and I'm sure you don't want to get under foot. Come with me. There's something I want to show you.'

Urbanus led the four friends off the track, up a dark stairwell and into the vast bright space of the seating. Here and there, slaves were sweeping the marble benches or using red paint to fill the shallow incisions that marked the seats, but mostly the great Circus was deserted.

As Urbanus led them higher and higher, Lupus noticed that the marble seats gave way to wooden benches on the upper levels. Finally they reached the highest tier, a roofed colonnade. The morning sun streaming through an arched window in the outer wall of the colonnade warmed his back as he turned to look down over the arena. From here they had a bird's-eye view of the whole Circus.

'Behold!' said Nubia. 'The middle thing is full of water, with temples and sculptures like islands.'

'Yes,' said Urbanus. 'Some people call the central barrier the spina, because it's like the backbone of the racecourse, but most call it the euripus.'

'Euripus means "canal",' said Nubia.

'That's right. They say the water in it represents the sea.'

Lupus chuckled, and pointed at the bronze dolphins.

'The racetrack surrounds the euripus,' continued Urbanus, 'just as the world surrounds the sea, so the racetrack represents the world. That obelisk there in the centre represents the sun. See the sun-shaped bronze flame on top? The twenty-four races are the hours of the day,' he continued, 'the seven laps the horses run are the seven days of the week, and the twelve gates of the carceres are the twelve months of the year.'

'Great Neptune's beard,' said Jonathan. 'Did they plan it that way?'

'They must have,' murmured Flavia. 'It couldn't be coincidence.'

'That's not all,' said Urbanus. 'The four colours of the factions represent the four seasons. Red is summer, Blue is autumn, White is winter and Green is spring. There's even an underground shrine to Consus, the god of storehouses, which is just like the entrance to Hades.'

Lupus stared at Urbanus in amazement and Flavia echoed his thoughts: 'Great Juno's peacock!' she breathed. 'I never knew that.'

'Life's a Circus,' said Urbanus. 'And the Circus is a world. Everything you need to know about life, you can learn right here in the Circus.'

Lupus glanced at Urbanus, and was surprised to see that his smiling eyes were moist with tears.

The Greens left the Circus Maximus at the third hour after dawn, just as the Whites were arriving for their test circuits. As they passed one another, the grooms and charioteers exchanged cheerful insults and laughter.

The Whites were followed into the hippodrome by a troop of curious-looking barbarians on shaggy ponies. They wore patterned trousers under short tunics and most had floppy cloth caps. Lupus guessed they were desultores, acrobats who jumped from horse to horse. The youngest was a hatless boy wearing zigzag-striped trousers under a vertically-striped tunic. He saw Lupus staring and gave him a grin.

Lupus tugged Flavia's tunic and pointed hopefully at the troupe passing into the hippodrome.

'You want to stay and watch the Scythians?' she said. He nodded.

Flavia hesitated. 'All right. You know where to find us. We're going back to the Stables of the Greens right now. Do you remember how to get there? Good. If Aristo comes here, remind him where we are. And don't forget the banquet later at Senator Cornix's. It's starting early, at the fourth hour after noon.'

Lupus nodded and grinned and ran after the acrobats.

Scopas was waiting for them in front of the Pavilion of the Greens. He was wearing his usual green tunic and a serious expression. 'Scopas wins the race,' he said. 'Maybe they will be kind to Scopas now.'

'Maybe who will be kind to you?' asked Nubia.

'But it was only a practice run,' added Scopas. 'So maybe it does not count.'

'Is is true?' said Jonathan. 'Do they run faster in a real race?'

'This is correct. They run faster in the real race.'

'Aren't you frightened when you race?' said Flavia. 'I was terrified.'

'Scopas is not afraid of horses. But sometimes Scopas is afraid of people.'

Suddenly Nubia caught sight of a familiar figure sitting by the bronze bull fountain. 'Flavia!' she whispered. 'Behold! It is the beggar who tells us where to find Sagitta. May I thank him?'

'Of course,' said Flavia. 'Let's go together.' She linked her arm in Nubia's and said over her shoulder to Jonathan and Scopas, 'We'll be right back.'

'Hello, again, sir,' said Nubia a moment later, letting her knees bend in respect. 'Thank you for helping us to find Sagitta yesterday.'

'Yes,' said Flavia. 'How did you know where to find him?'

The beggar smiled up at Nubia with dark intelligent eyes. 'I was passing the little Temple of Venus yesterday and I heard a horse whinny. I knew it was him.' He shook his head. 'I tried to tell others. But you were the only one to believe me.'

'Would you like to meet Urbanus?' Nubia gestured towards the Greens' pavilion. 'He might give you a reward, too.'

The beggar's smile faded and he hung his dark head. 'No. Urbanus hates me.'

'He hates you?' said Flavia.

'Yes,' muttered the beggar. 'He hates all cripples.'

'Do you want some of my gold then?' asked Nubia. 'I have much.'

'Nubia!' hissed Flavia. 'No!'

'Another denarius will do me fine.' He lifted his head and gave his gap-toothed grin. 'If I were rich I'd have no profession.'

Nubia stared at him wide-eyed. She had never heard of a beggar turning down gold. Was Jonathan's suggestion true? Could the one-legged beggar really be one of the gods in disguise?

*

Lupus watched the boy in zigzag trousers with a mixture of admiration and envy. The boy and his friends could vault onto their ponies, spin around, stand up and jump from one pony to the other, all while the creatures were moving.

Lupus had heard them talking to each other in a language that sounded like 'bar-bar-bar', and he guessed that few of them spoke Latin.

Presently a trumpet sounded and the desultores rode or led their mounts to the side of the carceres to watch the Whites run their practice circuits.

Lupus came down the steps from the front row of the seating, plonked himself on the sandy track beside the boy in zigzag trousers and grinned at him.

The boy grinned back. He had straight dark hair and dark almond-shaped eyes that slanted up at the corners.

Lupus pointed at the boy and at his shaggy pony and gave a thumbs-up, as if to say: You're good.

The boy nodded his thanks and his grin widened to show even white teeth.

Lupus pointed at the boy and then at himself and then at the pony.

Zigzag shook his head in puzzlement.

Lupus pointed at himself again. He forked the first two fingers of his right hand upside down and made them ride his left wrist. Then he pointed at the boy's pony.

'You want ride?' said Zigzag.

Lupus nodded vigorously.

'You know ride?'

Lupus shook his head, pointed at the boy and then at himself, and raised his eyebrows.

'You want teach ride?'

Lupus nodded again.

Zigzag grinned and shook his head. 'I too busy.'

But his eyes widened and his jaw dropped when Lupus reached into his belt-pouch and pulled out a bright gold coin, an aureus worth a hundred sesterces.

SCROLL X

The tenth time Lupus fell off the little shaggy pony, he groaned in frustration and angrily kicked at the sandy track.

'No,' said Zigzag patiently. 'Hold tight here.' He squatted and stroked the inside of his legs with both hands. 'You must have thighs of iron.'

Lupus gave his bug-eyed look and the boy laughed. 'Yes. Thighs of iron. Do not do this.' He flailed his arms wildly and waved his head about, mouth open and eyes rolling.

Lupus scowled at him, then took a deep breath and ran towards the pony.

He had easily mastered vaulting over the pony's rump and onto its low, sturdy back, and he could sit on it while it walked, but as soon as it began to trot he always fell off. This time he held his arms loosely by his side but clamped his thighs tightly round the pony's barrel body.

The pony began to trot and for a moment Lupus was tempted to grab wildly for its woolly mane. Instead he kept his arms relaxed and made his thighs grip like iron.

And he stayed on.

A huge grin spread across his face as the pony trotted in a circle around the boy.

The boy uttered a brief command and the pony began to gallop.

Once again, Lupus found himself on the sandy track of the Circus Maximus.

After the practice run in the hippodrome, Nubia hurried straight back to the Stables of the Greens. Flavia and Jonathan were eager to spend some of their reward money on gifts for friends and family, but she longed to be with Pegasus. She also wanted to know if Aristo was feeling better.

However, Aristo was not at the stables and she couldn't find Scopas either.

'Have you seen Scopas?' she asked one stable boy after another. Most shook their heads, but some snickered and a good-looking boy with blond hair spat contemptuously on the ground. 'Scopas is a freak,' he said. 'He thinks he can become an auriga when he hasn't even been here one month. He should be put up for sale in the Monster Market.'

Nubia finally found Scopas in a corner of Incitatus's stall, rocking and gently thumping his head against the frescoed wall. He was whimpering: 'Zip q'nee, zip q'nee, zip q'nee.'

He had been whipped and beaten, then tied up with green ribbons. As a final indignity, he had been smeared with horse manure.

'Great Juno's beard!' said Jonathan. 'He's been beaten.'

He and Flavia had arrived back at the Stables of the Greens to find Nubia sponging Scopas's face.

'Nubia, what happened?' Flavia dropped her parcels

in the doorway of the frescoed stall and ran forward. Jonathan followed.

'They beat him,' said Nubia.

'Who?' said Jonathan.

'I think stable boys,' said Nubia in a small voice.

'Some of the stable boys of the Greens did this?' gasped Flavia.

Nubia nodded, and waved away the flies buzzing round Scopas, who was sitting on the silken couch, staring blankly ahead and rocking.

'Does Urbanus know about this?' asked Flavia.

'I just heard!' Urbanus hurried through the doorway. 'One of the grooms told me – Master of the Universe! Look what they've done to him.' He knelt before Scopas and gently examined the boy's head and arms. Suddenly he turned and they followed his gaze to see a dozen sullen stable boys lurking outside the frescoed stall. Urbanus rose and stalked to the doorway. 'Did you do this?'

Most hung their heads but the blond stared back defiantly. 'We don't like him and we don't want him here.'

'You don't like him,' repeated Urbanus.

A few shook their heads.

'Any of you who don't like this boy,' he said, speaking softly and clearly, 'have my permission to leave these stables *immediately*! You can go and work for one of the other factions.' Urbanus was no longer speaking softly. 'Those of you who stay will treat him with respect!' He slammed the door on them and returned to Scopas. 'Jealous,' he muttered. 'Cruel and jealous.'

Scopas was still staring blankly ahead, and his lips were forming the silent words 'zip q'nee' over and over.

'What language is that?' asked Flavia.

'I don't know,' said Urbanus with a sigh. 'It's not Greek or Hebrew or Aramaic or any language I've ever heard of.' He shook his head. 'Maybe it *is* the language of centaurs.'

'What?'

'Centaurs. Man's torso, horse's body. I wrote to his people at Delphi shortly after he arrived and recently had a letter back from a priest there. He said they think Scopas was raised by centaurs.'

'Scopas was raised by centaurs?' repeated Flavia incredulously.

'That's what they said. They told me that he didn't speak until he was ten or eleven. Apparently he would sit rocking for hours, staring at a grain of sand or a wild flower. If anyone touched him he would fight and scream. Wouldn't be held, wouldn't be comforted, just banged his head against a wall. Seemed impervious to pain. But he always loved animals, especially horses.' Urbanus swatted at a fly. 'I suppose that's why they thought he was raised by centaurs.'

'What are you using to sponge his cuts?' Jonathan asked Nubia, glancing at her copper bowl.

'Vinegar,' said Nubia. 'Hippiatros gives it to me.'

Jonathan turned to Urbanus. 'Do you have baths here, sir? I should wash this muck off him before we anoint his wounds. My father's a doctor,' he added.

'Bless you, son.' Urbanus blinked back tears. 'I'd be very grateful if you would attend to the boy. The Baths of Agrippa are just past Pompey's Theatre, only a block away.' Urbanus reached into his belt-pouch and pulled out a coin. 'They're expensive but good. Here. Take this. Wash him and anoint him and bring him back here. I'll put him in my own apartment upstairs if that's what it takes to keep him safe.'

Scopas was not even allowed to enter the baths until a slave had sluiced him down with a bucket of warm water. Jonathan paid his coin and led Scopas into the apodyterium.

Jonathan peeled off Scopas's filthy tunic and handed it to a bath attendant, telling him to burn it and send someone out to buy a new one. Then he turned back to Scopas. He could see that some of the bruises on the boy's skinny torso were old ones. 'This isn't the first time they've beaten you,' he muttered, as he slipped off his own tunic.

Jonathan led Scopas to the caldarium and helped him down into a circular hot plunge. Scopas did not even flinch as he entered the steaming hot myrtle-scented water.

After a long soak, Jonathan guided Scopas carefully back up the marble steps and helped a slave to towel him off. They led him to the massage room and Jonathan asked the gentlest-looking slave to rub olive oil into the boy's bruised body. Jonathan knew Scopas did not like people to touch him, but the boy did not even flinch.

When the slave had finished a long, thorough massage, Jonathan anointed the cuts on Scopas's face and arms with vinegar. Again, the boy did not react. Finally, Jonathan dressed him in the new tunic he had sent the slave to buy. It was a man's tunic, not a boy's, and it made Scopas look small and vulnerable.

As Jonathan bent to lace up Scopas's sandals he

wondered what a terrible childhood the boy must have had.

'Urbanus,' said Scopas suddenly, and Jonathan looked up in surprise.

'What?'

'Scopas wants Urbanus—' his voice was as flat as ever '—and Pegasus.'

'Yes,' said Jonathan, standing up and extending his hand. 'Come on. I'll take you back to the stables. To Urbanus and your horse.'

'I want to offer a votive,' said Flavia later that day, 'for Scopas's recovery.'

It was afternoon, and the three friends were passing the medicine stalls on their way back to Senator Cornix's.

'What kind of votive?' asked Jonathan, shifting his parcels in his arms. 'What do you offer when you don't even know what's wrong with the person?'

'I'm not sure,' murmured Flavia, stopping to examine the objects on one of the stalls. 'I'll know it when I see it.' On the cloth before her were clay ears, eyes, noses, hands, feet, even little clay models of the private parts of both men and women.

'No,' murmured Flavia. 'None of those . . .' She moved onto the next stall and then the next and presently she uttered a cry of triumph. A moment later she returned with a little bronze model of a centaur.

'That must have cost a few sesterces,' said Jonathan. 'What are you going to do with it?'

'Offer it at the Temple of Aesculapius, of course,' said Flavia. 'Coming?'

Jonathan looked over at the Tiber Island, with its

red temple rooftops, green trees and white marble obelisk.

'No', he said with a shudder. 'I don't like that place. I'll wait for you in the Forum Boarium.'

'Any news?' asked Flavia half an hour later, as she and Nubia came up to Jonathan with their parcels. He was standing before a noticeboard near the Temple of Hercules.

Without turning Jonathan quoted, 'The Ludi Romani begin tomorrow. Two weeks of chariot races in honour of Jupiter. To be opened with a dawn sacrifice by the Pontifex Maximus at the Temple of Jupiter Stator.' He glanced at the hill rising above the forum. 'According to this, they usually have the sacrifice at the Temple of Jupiter on the Capitoline Hill,' he said, 'but it's still being repaired after the fire.'

'Oh.' Flavia and Nubia exchanged a quick look. They knew Jonathan blamed himself for the terrible fire six months before.

'We made an offering for Scopas,' said Flavia brightly.

'We also searched for Aristo,' said Nubia. 'But he was not there. Behold!' she whispered, her golden eyes suddenly wide.

Flavia followed her gaze and gasped. The one-legged beggar sat beside the round temple of Hercules, at the foot of one of its fluted, honey-coloured columns.

'I am sure he was not there a moment ago,' said Nubia. 'He appears as if by magic.'

The beggar was beckoning to them and despite the heat, Flavia felt a strange chill. 'Come on then,' she said, and a moment later she was standing before him, fishing in her coin purse for something smaller than a gold coin.

'No,' said One-leg. 'This time I want to give *you* something.' He held out a dark strip in his twisted left hand. Flavia shuddered to see the stumps where his last two fingers had been amputated. But she reached out and bravely took the strip from his hand. It was as long as her thumb but slightly wider. And surprisingly heavy.

'It's a lead tablet,' she said.

The beggar nodded. 'I just found it near the Stables of the Greens,' he said, 'beside a bound, headless rooster. I think it's a curse-tablet. You should warn them. They wouldn't listen to a humble beggar.'

Flavia frowned. 'The letters aren't Greek or Latin. I don't recognise the language.'

'The characters are Hebrew,' said Jonathan, looking over her shoulder, 'but the words are gibberish. May I see?'

Flavia handed him the tablet and after a few moments he looked up. 'It's Aramaic, but written backwards.' He glanced down at One-leg. 'It's a curse-tablet, all right.'

'Can you decipher it?' asked Flavia.

Jonathan nodded. '*As this cock is bound, legs, wings and body, I adjure you, O demons, by the Great God of the Heavens above, to bind the legs, hands and bodies of the charioteers of the Greens, and the horses they are going to drive, especially Bubalo, Glaucus, Sagitta and Latro. And I adjure you, by him who sits on the Cherubim, that you destroy Castor, Cresces, Antilochus, Gegas, Phoenix, Tatianus and Eutychus so that they might not greet Victory tomorrow but encounter Nemesis instead. Now. Now.*

Quick. Quick.' Jonathan turned the tablet over and then looked at the beggar. 'Where did you say you found this?' he asked.

'Buried in the dirt at the foot of the wall where I usually sit. Just outside the Stables of the Greens. It wasn't there yesterday,' he added.

'But who would do such a thing?' said Nubia.

'Maybe the same person,' said Flavia grimly, 'who abducted Sagitta and tortured him.'

SCROLL XI

'We have to warn Castor and the other charioteers about the curse-tablet,' said Flavia as they left the Forum Boarium.

'Are you mad?' said Jonathan. 'That would cause maximum panic.'

'But the beggar entrusted it to us.'

'There's something strange about that beggar,' said Jonathan.

'I am thinking you are right; that he is maybe a god in disguise,' said Nubia.

Jonathan stared at her. 'I was only joking when I said that. You can't really believe he's one of the gods?'

'Of course we don't,' said Flavia, 'but there *is* something mysterious about him. He always appears just when we need him.'

'I still don't think you should tell anyone about that tablet.'

'I thought you didn't believe in curses.'

'I don't. But my father says curses can be dangerous because some people really do believe them.'

'All right,' said Flavia. 'But if we don't warn the charioteers about the curse-tablet and something happens tomorrow, it will be on your head.'

*

Bulbus the door-slave greeted them with a vast grin.

'He's here!' he said in a stage whisper. 'Castor! The head trainer, too! Right here in the senator's house!'

Jonathan stared past the big slave in surprise. Flavia's uncle always grumbled about how Rome was sinking into a swamp of decadent luxury. But here was his atrium, festooned with smiling garlands of jasmine and ivy, and there was Sisyphus hurrying towards them with expensive, market-bought garlands for their heads.

Jonathan and Flavia handed their parcels to a slave and together with Nubia they followed Sisyphus into the shade-dappled inner garden.

'Flavia! Jonathan!' boomed Senator Cornix. He slid off one of the couches which had been arranged on a brick path around a bubbling fountain. 'Castor is here!' He gestured to the hawk-nosed man reclining on the central couch.

Jonathan stared. 'Great Juno's beard!' he muttered. 'I spent the morning hugging the greatest auriga of our time and I didn't even know it.'

Senator Cornix continued the introductions. 'And you know the head trainer.'

Urbanus reclined beside Lady Cynthia. Jonathan saw that the head trainer was freshly shaved and his long sandy hair pulled back in a ponytail.

'How is Scopas?' Jonathan asked him.

'Much better, thanks to you,' said Urbanus, and his eyes were smiling. 'He's sleeping in Pegasus's stall. I offered him my own bed but he wanted to stay with the horse. I think he'll be fine.'

'Praise Juno,' breathed Flavia, and then turned to her aunt. 'I'm so sorry we're late. Our friend was beaten and we stopped to offer a prayer for him.'

'You're not late,' said Lady Cynthia. 'You're just in time.' In addition to the flowered garland in her dark hair, Jonathan noticed she was wearing much more jewellery than she usually did.

'Is Lupus back?' he asked.

'Just now,' said Aulus Junior from the table. 'He's in the latrine.'

'And Aristo?' asked Nubia.

'Aristo!' muttered Jonathan to Flavia. 'I forgot all about him.'

'Aristo is resting in a darkened room,' said Cynthia. 'The wretched boy had a bad time with the tooth-puller so I called our physician to give him a dose of poppy-tears.'

'No wonder he never came back to the stables,' murmured Flavia.

'Poor Aristo,' said Nubia.

'Sit at the table, children,' said Senator Cornix. 'There's plenty of room for you all.'

Jonathan washed his hands in the bowl proffered by a slave-girl and sat at the table between Aulus Junior and Hyacinth. The gustatio was salty strips of brick-coloured ham – so thin they were translucent – wrapped around sweet green cubes of melon.

Castor the hawk-nosed charioteer winked at Jonathan. During the practice circuit earlier in the day, he had uttered only two words: 'Hang on.'

Now, bathed and fresh in a leek-green synthesis, and with a silver wine goblet in his hand, he became extremely loquacious, regaling them with tales of his adventures in the circus.

Beside Lady Cynthia, Urbanus sipped his wine and watched his star charioteer hold court.

'See this amulet?' said Castor, pulling a vicious-looking yellow tusk from the matted chest hair above the neck of his tunic.

Lady Cynthia uttered a polite exclamation: 'Mecastor!'

'It makes me brave as a boar,' laughed the charioteer, 'which is the creature it's taken from. This helps me feel powerful, too.' He took a twist of papyrus from his belt-pouch and poured a fine brown powder into his silver goblet. 'It's what all us charioteers drink. Combined with wine, it makes a powerful potion.' He held out his cup and Sisyphus skipped over to top it up. He was not the senator's usual wine-steward but Jonathan guessed he had asked to be allowed to wait on the banquet.

'Sisyphus, don't hover over our guest of honour,' grumbled Senator Cornix. 'Other people need refilling, too.'

'Anyone want to try some of my special potion?' said Castor. He stirred the wine with his meaty forefinger.

Jonathan raised an eyebrow. 'What's in the powder?'

'Same thing they smear on charioteers' wounds if they've been thrown or trampled.' Castor licked his finger and made the sign against evil. 'Boar's dung!'

'Mecastor!' yelped Sisyphus.

'No,' said the big charioteer. 'Me Castor!'

Everyone laughed and Castor took a long deep drink from his cup. 'Ahhhh!' He let out a theatrical sigh of pleasure and gave a textured burp. 'Life's a circus.'

Lupus pointed at Castor's goblet and shook his head and grunted no.

'What?' said Castor. 'You don't believe it's really boar's dung?'

Lupus folded his arms and shook his head.

'It's perfectly true,' said Castor cheerfully. 'This potion's made of powdered boar's dung. Nero himself used to drink such a brew. Makes you strong as an ox and brave as a boar. Come on, then!' He held out his goblet to Lupus. 'I dare you to try some.'

Lupus's chair scraped on the brick path as he pushed it away from the table and stood up. He marched over to Castor's couch and took the cup.

'Lupus!' cried Jonathan. 'No!'

Lupus glanced at him, scowled, and stared at the mixture. Then he took a deep breath and tipped the contents down his throat.

Everyone stared in horror as Lupus clutched his neck, and – eyes bulging – sank slowly to his knees.

Jonathan pushed back his chair as Lupus sank to the garden path.

But before he could run to his friend, Lupus sprang up again, a mischievous grin on his face. Everyone laughed as he adopted the pose of an athlete in the palaestra showing off his muscles.

Jonathan shook his head as Lupus handed Castor his silver goblet and rejoined his friends at the table.

Through the main course of roast goose and the dessert of peppered pear patina, Castor continued to regale them with stories about the life of a charioteer.

'I remember one horse,' he said, gesturing with a half-eaten wedge of patina, 'called Imperator. Imperator was an ex-cavalry horse. He was big and beautiful and as fast as a Roman legionary with a score of barbarian women on his tail. Everyone was convinced he'd be Rome's new champion.' Castor popped the last of the patina in his mouth. 'Only problem was, whenever

Imperator heard the trumpet, he bolted. He was terrified of that sound.'

Castor blared an imaginary trumpet, pretended to leap forward, and made his fingernails gallop across the fulcrum of his couch.

'Didn't matter where he was,' continued Castor, when their laughter subsided, 'in the opening procession, trotting out his lap of honour, going back to the stables . . . Whenever he heard that trumpet, Imperator bolted!'

Castor blared and his fingernails galloped. Lupus laughed so hard that wine spurted out of his nose.

'But then, one terrible day,' continued Castor in a dramatic whisper, 'disaster struck! They'd just loaded all the horses into the starting gates . . . and the trumpet sounded! Imperator was off! And slammed right into the closed wooden doors of the gate.' Castor slapped his forehead with the palm of his hand and imitated a horse slowly toppling over. 'Ah, yes,' he said. 'Life's a circus.'

Everyone was laughing except Urbanus, who gazed into his wine cup, apparently oblivious to everything around him. Jonathan fingered the lead tablet in his coin pouch. Should he tell the trainer about the curse? No. He was certain his first instinct was right; such information was bound to cause panic. Besides, he was sure that nothing would come of it.

It is night when the chimera comes to burn the tents with its hot breath of hatred. Nubia rides Pegasus across the dark sand towards her family's tent. But the tent is no longer made of goatskin. It is made of fire. She knows she and Pegasus must jump through the flames to save the person trapped inside. But who?

Ever since she first saw Pegasus in Surrentum she has dreamt this dream. This nightmare.

She knows she is dreaming but she can never change it.

Or can she?

She remembers what Flavia said. Imagine Pegasus is a winged horse. Imagine he can fly.

'Fly!' she cries out to him in her dream. 'Fly!'

And now the sand dunes are falling away below them and they are rising above the flames and she can hear the great whoosh of his wings and feel the breeze on her face. They are in the night sky, passing over the tent, and as Nubia looks down she sees a face looking up. For the first time since the slave-traders burnt their tents, her dream almost allows her to see the person she failed to save.

Early the next morning Senator Cornix led his household in the predawn ritual of the Nones. Flavia and the others stood yawning in the torchlit atrium, facing the senator as he washed his hands before the household shrine. Even Aristo was there, smelling strongly of clove-oil and pressing a poultice to his swollen jaw.

It was chilly, so Flavia pulled her new leaf-green palla closer around her shoulders; she was wearing it in honour of the Greens. Nubia had one just like it. Jonathan, Lupus and Aulus each wore a scarlet-edged toga praetexta, with green tunics underneath. Lady Cynthia and her three younger children were also present. Hyacinth and the twins had runny noses and kept sniffing.

The senator dried his hands on a folded towel, sprinkled powdered incense onto the glowing coals of a small brazier and covered his head with a fold of his own toga, lit golden by the flickering torches. Then he stood for a moment in solemn silence. Flavia's nostrils flared at the spicy scent of frankincense and cinnamon, a scent which always evoked early mornings standing before the lararium in her own home.

'Salve, O Janus, bringer of the new day,' intoned senator Cornix. 'Salve, O goddess Juno who gives us health and protection. Salvete, O Lares and Penates, and you, O Genius of the household.' After each 'salve' he made the gesture of adoratio, kissing his fingertips and stretching out his open hand, then sprinkling a little more powder on the coals.

A sudden eddy of incense filled Flavia's head, prickling her nose and making her want to sneeze. She stifled it by pinching her nostrils. She knew that if she sneezed or laughed or even coughed, the whole ritual might have to be repeated. Furthermore, it would be a bad omen, and with the terrible curses of that tablet hanging over the Greens, a bad omen was the last thing they needed.

The senator continued, 'Salve, goddess Vesta, guardian of hearth and home.' He took a small cake from a three-legged table near the lararium. 'As I give you this loaf of grain, do you likewise give health and happiness to me and to my familia.' He touched his chest, kissed his fingertips and gestured around the atrium.

Flavia looked up at the dark rectangle of sky above the impluvium; the stars were fading.

'Salvete, O Castor and Pollux,' continued her uncle, 'divine twins and sons of Jove. Salve, O Jupiter Pater, on this your special day please bless us and our Imperator Titus.'

At the mention of 'Imperator', Flavia remembered Castor's imitation of the charging racehorse and she almost giggled. Instead she bit her lower lip hard, acutely aware of Lupus shaking with silent laughter beside her.

'If anything of this ritual or offering is displeasing,' the senator was saying, 'then receive this incense of atonement.' Here he sprinkled a final dusting onto the coals. 'I, Aulus of the gens Caecilia, surnamed Cornix, receive on behalf of myself and my familia all that is good and pure and noble and right.' The senator faced the lararium, pinched out the candle flame on the altar and uncovered his head.

'Well done, everyone,' he said. 'Let us go in peace and protection to enjoy the races of Father Jupiter.'

Flavia breathed a sigh of relief: the ceremony had gone without a hitch. But as they filed past the lararium, her heart skipped a beat. In passing the small shrine, Aulus Junior jostled it and one of the divine twins toppled over onto his face. As Flavia quickly stood the little effigy upright, her stomach did a strange flip. Even in the flickering torchlight she could see the fallen twin was Castor.

Usually the races started shortly after dawn, but on this, the first day of Ludi Romani, the emperor was sacrificing to the Father of the gods at the Temple of Jupiter Stator near the Forum and the Palatine Hill.

The first race would not begin until mid-morning so Senator Cornix had given Flavia and her friends permission to see how Scopas was doing. By the time the four friends reached the Stables of the Greens it was light, though the sun had not yet appeared over the rooftops.

They showed their wristbands to the yawning guard by the green marble columns, and made their way through the bustling atrium to the stable courtyard. Nubia was alarmed to see a group of stable boys looking over the half-door of Pegasus's stall, and she ran forward.

The boys dispersed when they saw her approaching; she dreaded what she might see.

It was worse than she could have imagined.

Golden-maned Pegasus lay motionless on the hay. And crushed between the horse's dark back and the masonry stall divider was the body of a boy: Scopas.

SCROLL XII

'It's all right, Nubia!' cried Flavia. 'They're alive. Look!'

Nubia uncovered her eyes, and sobbed with relief. Scopas was helping Pegasus to his feet. A moment later, the horse put his beautiful head over the wooden door of his stall, and Nubia threw her arms around his neck. 'Oh, Pegasus!' she cried. 'I thought you were dead. You also,' she said to Scopas.

His face was bruised from his beating the day before, but somehow his expression seemed softer.

'Do not be vexed,' he said, and his voice was softer, too. 'Scopas asked Pegasus to do this. It is very blue.'

'Blue?' said Flavia. 'What do you mean "blue"?'

'It is calming.'

'Calming?' yelped Jonathan. 'It's calming to have an enormous racehorse lying on top of you?'

'He does not lie on top of Scopas,' said Scopas. 'He squeezes Scopas firmly against the wall. It is comforting. It is blue.'

'I've never seen a horse lying down,' said Flavia. 'Except for a dead horse once.'

'Pegasus likes to lie down,' said Scopas. 'And he does not mind when Scopas lies beside him.'

'Under him, more like,' muttered Jonathan.

'Sabotage!' shouted Urbanus, coming up behind them. 'Someone has taken their idols.'

'Idols?' said Flavia.

'Effigies. Statues of their gods. We were about to take them over to our pavilion, but they've gone. My charioteers are panicking, the superstitious creatures!' He glared around at them. 'I don't suppose any of you have seen them?'

The four friends shook their heads, and then jumped as Urbanus struck his green whip hard against a stable door.

'By all the—!' He took a deep breath. 'Listen: if you want to make yourselves useful, have a look for them in these stalls. Then start grooming the horses. Half the stable boys ate bad figs last night and will be spending the day in the public latrines. Master of the Universe! What a disaster!' He stalked off, shaking his head.

When he was out of earshot, Jonathan turned to Scopas. 'Did you take the idols? Or give the stable boys bad figs?' he whispered. 'As revenge for beating you?'

'No,' said Scopas, and Nubia could see his confusion was genuine. 'Why would Scopas take idols or give bad figs?'

Jonathan shrugged and helped the others search the stalls for idols. They found nothing but horse manure and presently Scopas said, 'We must groom the horses, as Urbanus requests. Nubia and Flavia, you brush Pegasus's mane and tie in the ribbons. Jonathan, you brush Bubalo. Lupus, you brush Latro. I will show you how.'

'Does the Pegasus race today?' Nubia asked Scopas, picking up a curry-comb.

'No, but Urbanus will ride him in the pompa, the opening procession.'

Nubia took a pitted date from her coin-pouch and fed it to Pegasus. 'No, Flavia,' she said, 'do not pat him like that. Stroke him like this.'

'He's so big,' said Flavia, tentatively running her hand along his arched neck. 'Doesn't he frighten you?'

'No,' said Nubia. 'I can feel he is excited but calm. Can you not feel that when you stroke him?'

'No. I only feel nervous of him. But I'm going to see if he'll talk to me like he talks to you. How do you do it?'

'Make your mind still and smooth like a grey pebble.'

'Why grey?'

'I do not know. It seems right. Make your mind smooth and touch him. Then he will show you how he feels in pictures or feelings.'

'I'm going to try,' said Flavia. She closed her eyes and tentatively stroked Pegasus's satiny flank.

Presently she opened her eyes and shook her head. 'Nothing,' she said. 'I didn't get a picture.'

'It is not picture like fresco on the wall,' said Nubia. 'Sometimes it is dim and fuzzy. Here, I will help you.' She put her hand on Pegasus's neck and immediately saw the fleeting image of a hooded figure bending over a chariot.

'That is strange,' murmured Nubia. 'He usually shows me burning tent.'

'Hey, Scopas!' called Jonathan from two stalls down. 'Why do they have those strips of cloth wound around their legs?'

'Urbanus says their lower forelegs are easily bruised,' came Scopas's voice, still softer than usual. 'The cloth strengthens and protects their legs. Sometimes the cloth holds a poultice in place.'

'What's a poultice?' asked Flavia.

'Any kind of medicinal paste smeared on cloth,' said Jonathan from his stall. In the stall next to him Lupus stood on an upturned wooden bucket and carefully brushed Latro's mane.

'Have you seen my god?' came a man's quavering voice and they all looked up to see the African charioteer looking over the half-door of Pegasus's stall. Nubia saw that his handsome ebony face was wet with tears.

'I am sorry, Phoenix,' said Scopas. 'Your god is not here.'

'Poor Phoenix,' murmured Nubia, after the African had left. 'I wonder who took his god.' Pegasus blew softly through his nostrils and once again she had the vague image of a hooded figure bending over a chariot. She looked up at Pegasus and saw that he had turned his head to regard her with an intelligent eye.

'Scopas,' she said, 'where do you keep chariots?'

'Over there. You can see them from here. In that room off the courtyard.'

Nubia put down the curry-comb and went out of the stall. Scopas and Flavia followed her across the courtyard and into a corridor-like room with a row of wicker and leather chariots along a red-panelled wall. Cartwrights were checking the alignment of wheels and oiling the axles with animal fat. The two chariots on the far end were covered with canvas tarpaulins and cobwebs. Nubia went to the furthest chariot and pulled back the protective cloth.

'Those two have to be repaired,' said one of the cartwrights. 'They won't be used today.'

'What have you found?' said Scopas.

Nubia turned and lifted out a small bronze statue of a man with a dog's head. In the chariot were half a dozen other small figures in bronze or stone.

'You found them!' squealed Flavia, her eyes wide. 'You found the stolen gods. Phoenix! Castor! Antilochus! We found your gods.'

'My sacred image!' Phoenix ran up as they emerged back into the early morning light of the courtyard. He grasped a statuette of Hercules and gave Nubia a kiss on the forehead. 'You found my sacred image! Oh praise Jupiter, Juno and Minerva!'

Six other charioteers ran up and took their idols with thanks and tears of gratitude. Castor claimed a little marble statue of the goddess Fortuna, while a bald Egyptian took the dog-headed statue and then bent to kiss Nubia's toes where they emerged from her sandals. She giggled, but her smile faded when Urbanus came up to her.

'How did you know where to find those?' he said angrily.

Nubia did not know what to say.

'How?' shouted Urbanus. 'HOW?' He struck his whip hard against one of the columns of the peristyle.

'Pegasus is telling me!' said Nubia. 'He shows me image of man in hood by these chariots. I come to look and I find them.'

'The *horse* told you?' Urbanus glared at her for a

moment, then snorted. His long sandy hair swung as he turned on his heel.

Nubia felt tears prick her eyes. Why was Urbanus angry with her? She had found his drivers' lucky images. Surely he should be pleased.

It was the third hour after sunrise. Soldiers lined the road all the way from the Campus Martius to the Circus Maximus. They held back the cheering crowds as horses, charioteers, medics and sparsores proceeded towards the hippodrome, where they would join the emperor for the great pompa. Nubia and her three friends were walking near the front of the procession beside Pegasus and Scopas.

'Why is Urbanus angry with me?' Nubia asked Flavia. 'I find their gods.'

'I don't know,' said Flavia, raising her voice to be heard above the cheers of the crowd.

Jonathan leaned in as he walked. 'I think Urbanus was frustrated with the charioteers,' he said, 'because they're so superstitious.'

'But he also seemed angry with Nubia,' said Flavia.

Lupus nodded his agreement, and side-stepped to avoid a steaming pile of horse manure.

'Maybe he thinks Nubia was the one who hid the idols and only pretended to find them again,' suggested Jonathan, 'to get attention. Or to gain his favour.'

'Maybe,' said Flavia.

'These charioteers are certainly very popular.' Jonathan brushed rose-petals out of his curly hair.

'More than gladiators,' agreed Flavia.

'Or beast-fighters,' said Nubia.

'Greens, we love you!' squealed a pretty young woman in the crowd.

'They love us,' said Jonathan, looking pleased.

'You Greens are rubbish!' yelled a short man in a blue tunic.

'Well, maybe not all of them.'

'Rubbish,' repeated the man in blue. The rising sun made his face seem blood red. 'You cheat! You've never won a fair race in your history—' His tirade was cut short as several men in green tackled him and brought him thudding down onto the hard paving stones. Immediately, half a dozen soldiers ran forward to separate them.

Flavia nodded. 'Uncle Aulus says the Greens and the Blues often have fights. He says the Blues usually start it. Sometimes people get killed!'

As they passed through the arch of the city gate, Nubia could see the four pavilions of the factions among the temples of the Forum Boarium, with the Circus Maximus rising up behind, bright in the morning sun. The clip-clop of the horses' hooves seemed to pick up speed and her own heart was beating fast with excitement.

There were guards and barriers to keep the public out of the Forum Boarium, but it was still packed with horses, charioteers and grooms; everyone would take part in the opening ceremony.

They were just passing the bronze bull fountain when Nubia heard shouts. She looked over to see Urbanus beating the one-legged beggar with the handle of his green leather whip. 'I've told you to stay away from here!' shouted Urbanus. 'Get out!'

The beggar whimpered, and shielded his head with

his twisted arms. He held his copper begging-beaker in one hand.

'Stop!' cried Nubia, running to stand between Urbanus and the beggar. She held up her hands. 'Do not hurt him! He is just a wretched beggar!'

Urbanus's eyes blazed and for a moment she thought he might strike her, too. Instead, he turned and stalked into the pavilion without a backward glance.

'Sisyphus!' cried Flavia, half an hour later, as they reached Senator Cornix's seats. 'What's that thing on your head?'

'It's not a *thing*,' he replied stiffly. 'It's an umbrella hat. Keeps the sun off my face.'

'But we're in the shade. That's why these seats are so good.'

'Easier to wear it than hold it,' said Sisyphus, 'and we won't be in the shade for ever.'

Looking around, Nubia saw a few other umbrella hats dotted among the buzzing spectators, especially the rich and fashionable ones down here by the track.

'They're the latest fashion,' said Sisyphus proudly.

Senator Cornix had some of the best seats in the Circus: on the front row at the southwestern end of the Circus Maximus, in the shade for most of the morning. The seats were between the meta prima – where the most exciting manoeuvring took place – and the finishing line.

Just to Nubia's right, down on the track, was the tiny temple of Murcia with its sacred myrtle bush. Most of the charioteers hugged the central barrier at this point and were in no danger of colliding with it. Even so,

Nubia thought it strange to have a shrine right on the track itself.

Lady Cynthia had stayed at home with her younger children, who had runny noses. Since the loss of her two babies in a plague, she took no chances. Only the eldest child – twelve-year old Aulus Junior – had been allowed to come. He sat beside his father on an aisle seat. On Senator Cornix's right was Sisyphus in his umbrella hat with Flavia beside him. Then came Nubia. Jonathan and Lupus sat on her right.

The seats were cold marble, hard and narrow, but Sisyphus had brought cushions for everyone to sit on, and parasols for when the sun rose higher. If Nubia sat squarely on the bench, she could feel the knees of the person behind digging into her back, so she moved forward and rested her feet in the grating of the bronze railing before her.

She remembered sitting here a year before, when they had followed Jonathan to Rome but had been unable to find him. She remembered the procession, like the one on the track below her now. That procession had marked the last day of the races; this one celebrated the first day.

As before, the Emperor Titus led the pompa. A quarter of Rome's million inhabitants cheered him as he drove through an arch to the left of the carceres and into the vast arena. Although the triple disaster of volcano, plague and fire had marred his first year as emperor, he was still popular. Nubia saw that he was not riding a light racing-chariot, but a much sturdier ceremonial version, strong enough to bear his bulk and also the weight of a gold and ivory statue – his boyhood friend Britannicus.

Just as he passed beneath them, Titus glanced up and Nubia saw his eyes widen in recognition. He gave them the merest nod, but he did not smile, for the procession of the gods was a solemn one.

'His hair's getting thin on top,' said Sisyphus, as the emperor passed by. 'You can see his bald spot clearly from up here.'

'He should get an umbrella hat,' remarked Jonathan drily.

'He's put on weight since last spring,' said Flavia.

'He is looking tired,' said Nubia.

'Pressure of running an empire,' said Senator Cornix.

Behind Titus came the statues of various gods, each cheered by their own special supporters or guilds: Victory, Neptune, Mars, Apollo, Jupiter, Juno, Minerva, Venus, and the heavenly twins. Some statues reclined on litters carried by acolytes. Others were driven in chariots by different faction drivers. Nubia knew that when the statues had completed a circuit of the course they would be set in the pulvinar, a covered box in the stands on the Palatine side of the hippodrome. Sometimes the Emperor sat there, too.

'Yo! Castor and Pollux!' Flavia clapped as effigies of the twins passed in a triumphal chariot below them. 'Long live the Gemini.'

Musicians and dancers were passing below, but their music was drowned out by a wave of sound which began at the far end of the hippodrome and rose to an almost unbearable crescendo: the first faction was entering the arena.

'Veneti!' screamed the crowd, 'Go Blues!'

Presently the cries changed to 'Albati!' and 'Russati!' as the Whites and Reds entered the hippodrome.

Finally came the biggest cheer of all: 'Prasini! Greens!'

A strange sound filled the arena, like the sound of a vast herd of thundering creatures.

'What is it?' cried Nubia.

'Roof tiles!' cried Aulus Junior. 'You clap your hands but keep them hollow, like roof tiles. It's the highest type of applause.'

Nubia looked around. Sure enough, everyone was clapping with cupped hands. Nubia tried roof-tile clapping, too, and laughed at the strangeness of it.

And now she found she was cheering as the factions passed beneath them. Horses, charioteers, trainers, medics, veterinarians, sparsores and acrobats: all wore their colours as they marched in the pompa. Strips of linen had been used to bind some of the horses' lower legs in blue, white, red or green. Ribbons of the same colour tied up their silky manes and made their tails into neat balls. Some of the horses of the Whites even had pearls woven into their manes. Lucky charms dangled from the necks of both horses and charioteers.

As the factions processed around the long sandy track, three priests sacrificed a ram on an altar of the central barrier. Smoke was rising from this altar by the time the Greens passed below them. A surge of pride swept over Nubia as she saw Urbanus riding Pegasus at the very front.

'What's the name of that superb dark horse with the golden mane and tail?' she heard a man behind her say. 'He's magnificent!'

'I don't know,' came the deeper voice of his companion. 'Never seen a horse like that before.'

Nubia turned around and saw two middle-aged men

in scarlet-bordered togas looking down at her with interest. 'Pegasus,' she said proudly and had to say it again in a shout to be heard above the roar of the crowd: 'He is Pegasus!'

SCROLL XIII

By the time the opening rituals and sacrifices had been completed, and Titus had taken his seat in the columned gallery above the starting gates, it was the beginning of the fourth hour of a glorious autumn morning. Flavia's stomach was churning and she couldn't decide if it was with excitement or dread. She took a deep breath and looked around the hippodrome.

'The first race,' said Senator Cornix, 'is between four bigae from each faction.'

'That makes it a sixteen-chariot race,' calculated Jonathan.

Lupus nodded and flashed a number with his hands, as he did in maths lessons with Aristo.

'That's right, Lupus,' said Jonathan. 'Thirty-two horses.'

'Will Sagitta run?' asked Flavia.

'He usually runs in a four-horse team,' explained Senator Cornix.

Sisyphus flapped a piece of papyrus. 'According to the programme,' he said, 'the alpha team isn't due to run until after lunch.'

'Behold!' Nubia pointed to a fenced-off area in the stands by the finishing line on her left. It was just below a small temple built into the seating. A low marble parapet separated some official-looking men from those in the seats around, while still allowing them to sit in plain view of the spectators.

'Those are stewards, and that's the finishing box,' said Senator Cornix.

Nubia nodded. She could see sixteen charioteers in four colours mounting steps straight from the racetrack up to this box. 'Behold!' she cried again. 'There is Castor!'

Jonathan nodded and grinned. 'It's Castor all right. I'd recognise that hawk nose anywhere.'

Lupus imitated drinking boar's dung potion and crossed his eyes.

'Yes,' murmured Sisyphus. 'Let's hope he's had his power potion today.'

'Oh, look at that blue charioteer!' cried Flavia. 'He has sweet little wings on his helmet.'

'He calls himself Hermes,' said Aulus Junior. 'He's *supposedly* the best charioteer of the Blues.' Aulus spat over the railing onto the track. 'He thinks he's a god.'

'Behold! Charioteers have balls!' cried Nubia.

Lupus guffawed and nodded enthusiastically.

Senator Cornix turned to Nubia. 'They're choosing lots,' he explained, 'to see who picks a gate first.'

Each charioteer handed a coloured ball to the man in the toga. When he had put them in a large revolving urn, a blindfolded slave reached in and pulled out the first ball. It was green. The crowd cheered as if the Greens had already won the race and Flavia saw Castor punch the air in triumph. She suddenly remembered the fallen image of Castor in the lararium, and her stomach twisted unpleasantly.

'That means Castor or one of his teammates gets first

choice of starting gate,' explained Sisyphus. 'That will give the Greens a good advantage. Flavia, are you all right? You look as pale as parchment!'

Flavia shook her head. 'I suddenly have a bad feeling about this.'

'Don't worry.' Sisyphus patted her arm. 'The first ball out of the urn was green. That's bound to be a good omen for all of us.'

Disaster struck the Greens in the first race.

It had not begun well. Titus had dropped the white mappa from his position over the carceres, the trumpets had uttered a long bright blast and the starting gates had sprung open. The thirty-two horses and their sixteen chariots thundered out to deafening applause but the Whites made a break for the inside lane before they reached the linea alba. This was not permitted, and the trumpets blasted the staccato signal for recall; the horses had to be reined in and driven back to the stalls.

Again the mappa fell, again the trumpets played the sustained starting note and the doors of the carceres opened, all except for the right-hand gate of one of the Reds; it had stuck closed.

Once again the trumpets stuttered their recall and then for a third time blared a long note as the mappa fell.

This time all the gates opened and the teams kept to their lanes until the chalk line of the linea alba. Castor and a pair of magnificent black stallions took the lead on the inside lane, while behind him two of his team-mates did their best to prevent the other bigae from overtaking.

'Brilliant!' cried Aulus. 'Those two Greens are using the pincer tactic.'

'What is that?' asked Nubia.

'That's when they come together to squeeze out other chariots,' explained Senator Cornix, 'and force the competition to either drop back or take an outside lane, both of which will slow them down.'

'Good teamwork,' murmured Jonathan, as the chariots disappeared around the meta prima in a spray of sand.

Boys in the colours of the four factions ran out to sprinkle something on the track.

'Who are they?' asked Nubia.

'Those must be the sparsores,' said Flavia. 'The sprinkly boys.'

'That's right,' said Senator Cornix. 'Their job is to sprinkle water on the track, to keep it from getting too dusty, and to spray the horses with water if they get overheated. They also have to remove any objects that might trip up the horses. It's quite a dangerous job,' he added. 'The year before last I saw two sparsores trampled to death.'

Nubia shuddered.

As the chariots rounded the far meta and raced up the straight for the second time, Castor was still in the lead. A steward on the track by the little shrine of Murcia flourished a green handkerchief as the chariots thundered past. This meant the Greens were ahead, and the crowd went wild.

By the fifth lap Castor and his team of green-ribboned black stallions were still in the lead as his teammates successfully blocked his rivals. The crowd had settled down for the tense middle section of the race and the roar subsided to a rumble, low enough for Nubia to hear a baby crying somewhere and a woman cheering the Reds and the piercing trill of a flute.

Suddenly – and for no apparent reason – Castor's biga gave such a burst of speed that he was jerked over the top of his chariot.

With a unanimous gasp, the entire circus rose to its feet. Castor had fallen heavily on the wooden pole of the yoke. This pole had snapped in two and now he was being dragged along the course by two panicking horses.

'Man overboard!' cried one of the senators behind Nubia.

All over the stands, men groaned and women screamed.

Flavia was gripping Nubia's arm so hard that it hurt. 'That black stallion has gone berserk!' she cried. 'Castor will be killed! Why doesn't he let go of the reins!'

'He can't let go,' said Jonathan grimly. 'Remember? The reins are tied round his waist. He'll have to cut himself free.'

As Castor's horses dragged him around the meta and out of sight, his empty chariot slowed and toppled over onto the sandy track.

'I can't see him!' cried Flavia. 'What's happening?'

'Don't ask us,' snapped Aulus Junior. 'None of us on this side can see.'

Suddenly there was a cry from a hundred thousand spectators on the other side of the hippodrome.

'These stupid front row seats!' cried Aulus Junior. 'We'd be able to see if we were up higher.'

'What is it?' cried Nubia. 'What's happened?'

The answer came a moment later, carried around the

arena by a wave of exclamations: a Red sparsor on the other side of the euripus had tried to slow the runaway horses and had been trampled.

'If Castor can just hang on a little longer,' said Senator Cornix from between clenched teeth, 'loose horses usually slow down and run for the exit. They'll catch them there.'

They saw the rest of the field thunder past on the other side of the barrier, and then two track assistants ran forward with a stretcher. For a moment they were lost to sight behind the euripus. Presently they reappeared with the body of a boy on their stretcher.

The crowd uttered an involuntary cry of alarm and Nubia turned to see that Castor's horses had not slowed down for the exit. Here they were – led by the foaming black stallion – rounding the meta secunda and turning for their sixth lap.

With a thrill of horror, Nubia saw that they were still dragging Castor.

'By Hercules!' cried Senator Cornix. 'I've never seen anything like this in all my life! Dragged for over half a circuit . . .'

'Juno's peacock!' gasped Sisyphus. 'He's alive! Look! He's still trying to cut himself free of the reins!'

'Oh, the poor man!' cried Flavia and covered her eyes.

Further along their row, a woman screamed and collapsed into her husband's arms. Even the swifts wheeling in the blue sky overhead seemed to shriek in horror.

As the horses came closer, Nubia saw that the inside stallion's eyes were rolling and his beautiful black flanks were covered with sweat. She had never seen such fear in a horse.

A moment later, the crowds around her gasped, then cheered. Castor had cut the last of the leather reins and had rolled to a stop, exhausted and bloody. His black horses ran on, trailing severed reins and a splintered wooden pole behind them.

But now there was another danger. The remaining chariots were still contesting the prize and they were heading straight for the battered figure lying on the track.

Medics quickly ran out with a wood and canvas stretcher and lifted Castor onto it. The crowd shrieked as the other chariots thundered towards them. Then a great cheer split the air. The medics had carried Castor out of the way with only a heartbeat to spare. Fifteen chariots raced on towards the turning point, with a group of five in the lead: a White first, then a Red, two Greens, and a Blue. They had one more lap to complete.

The sparsores had removed Castor's broken chariot from the racetrack but one of them must have missed a fragment of debris. As the lead White chariot neared the meta, it suddenly struck something, bounced into the air and crashed down onto its side.

More screams pierced the air, for the Red team had no time to take evasive action. In a flurry of horses' legs and spinning wheels, Nubia heard a sickening crack and a horse's scream.

'Naufragium!' cried the crowd. 'Shipwreck!' – and a quarter of a million Romans gave a great gasp of relief as the other chariots managed to steer around the tangle of wheels and legs.

Nubia covered her ears. She could not bear to hear the injured horses screaming. How could the Romans do such things? How could they be so cruel?

Down at the far end of the hippodrome, the sparsores and track officials had finally succeeded in subduing Castor's runaway pair, and Nubia thought she could see Urbanus running towards them.

'I must go,' she said to Flavia. 'I must find out what frightens black stallion.'

'I'll go with you,' said Flavia. She looked sick.

Lupus grunted and pointed at himself.

'Me, too,' said Jonathan miserably. 'This is partly my fault.'

Flavia and her friends squeezed along the row and hurried down some narrow steps. A low metal railing prevented direct access to the track, but a vaulted passageway led back under the seating to the arcades and road beyond. From there they ran up towards the Forum Boarium. The guards checked their wristbands and let them in just as a dozen Etruscan acrobats were riding through the arch and into the arena.

On this side of the carceres, they saw grooms from the four factions helping the charioteers into the chariots. The next race would consist of eight quadrigae. Flavia saw that Cresces was one of the two Green charioteers participating. His face was white as chalk.

In the Pavilion of the Greens, they found a crowd of charioteers and grooms standing around Castor, still on his stretcher. Urbanus was there, and the veterinarian Hippiatros, who was bending over the battered man, smearing a brown paste on his bloody legs.

'Praise the gods,' said Castor, lifting a steaming cup in a toast towards Nubia. Flavia could smell spiced wine. 'If you hadn't found my dear Fortuna, she would have deserted me. I was lucky today.'

'You call that lucky?' said Jonathan, staring at the battered and bloody charioteer.

'Of course,' continued Castor, 'dragged around the hippodrome and not one bone broken? If the African girl hadn't found my goddess, I'd have finished the race of life. As it is, poor Diomedes of the Whites reached that final goal first. I was lucky. Ah! Life's a circus.'

'I think you mean "death's a circus",' muttered Jonathan.

'You may not have broken any bones,' said Hippiatros, looking up from sponging Castor's bloody thigh, 'but you have extensive bruises, a twisted ankle, cracked ribs and half the skin torn off your body. I'm afraid you won't be riding any more chariots for the rest of the Ludi Romani.'

'Wool fluff!' said Castor with a chuckle. 'I'll be fine. Just smear some more of that boar's dung on me and – ow!' This last as Hippiatros began to bandage his right leg.

'Master of the Universe!' muttered Urbanus. 'My best auriga out of action on the first race.'

'Sir.' Jonathan cleared his throat and glanced hesitantly at Flavia. She gave him a firm nod. 'Sir, we have something to show you.'

Urbanus scowled at him. 'What?'

Jonathan reached into his coin purse and pulled out the curse-tablet.

'For God's sake, boy!' Urbanus tugged Jonathan

away from the men crowding around Castor. 'Get that thing out of sight!'

'You know what this is?' whispered Jonathan.

'Everyone knows what those are. If my men see that, we're finished.'

'Don't you want to know what's written on it?' said Flavia as Jonathan put the curse-tablet back into his coin-pouch.

'I can guess!' said Urbanus in an angry whisper. 'Invocation of some foreign demons to cripple and maim me, my horses and my drivers. Am I correct?'

Flavia gave a tiny nod.

'If my charioteers get the merest sniff of a curse-tablet, they'll panic and expect disaster. And when people expect something, it often comes to pass. In this faction I don't allow my charioteers to curse or be cursed.' Urbanus turned to Jonathan. 'You were foolish to bring that here, boy. Very foolish.'

Jonathan opened his mouth, glanced at Flavia, then closed it again.

'Sir?' said Nubia.

'Now what?' snapped Urbanus.

'May I see black stallion who goes berserk? I think I know what frightens him.'

'Oh you do, do you? Have the horses been talking to you again? Or did you read it on a curse-tablet?' He looked at her with blazing eyes. 'Get out of here, all of you, and take your occult superstition with you.'

'Sorry, Jonathan,' said Flavia as they squeezed between knees and the railing, back to their seats. 'I was certain he would want to see the tablet. Or at least hear the names. But you were right. He didn't want to know.'

'Because he didn't want to panic his men.' Jonathan resumed his seat beside Flavia.

A long blare of trumpets made them jump and eight quadrigae burst out of the carceres.

'Do they race again so soon?' asked Nubia. 'After such a terrible calamity?'

'Of course!' said Senator Cornix. 'They have eighteen races to get through today, and twenty-four on all the other days of the festival. Now, in a race like this, strategy and teamwork are of the utmost importance. See how that leading Green chariot is setting a blistering pace? He hopes the rest of the field will try to keep up. They'll be exhausted by the sixth lap and his Green teammate, who is cruising along at the back, can come in for an easy win.'

'Unless the wheel comes off,' muttered Jonathan. 'Like that!'

A lone wheel rolled lazily across the track and the crowd gasped as a chariot toppled onto its side. Miraculously, the charioteer had managed to remain upright on the lopsided chariot, which careened along in a spray of sand. The crowd cheered as the driver frantically tried to slow his team. His actions were almost comical and many were laughing.

But their laughter suddenly turned to gasps as he lost his footing and tumbled onto the track.

'Mecastor!' squealed Sisyphus.

'It's happening again!' cried Flavia and looked at Nubia in horror. 'He's being dragged along the track.'

Jonathan cupped his hands around his mouth. 'Cut yourself free!' he bellowed.

But the charioteer was as limp as a rag doll as he bounced along on the end of his reins.

'Why doesn't he cut himself free like Castor did?' cried Flavia.

'Maybe he can't.' Senator Cornix's voice was grim. 'He looks unconscious.'

'Oh! That Blue team is coming up too close! Can't they see him? Why don't they go around? Oh! I can't bear to look!' Flavia covered her eyes with her fingers. A moment later she heard the collective groan of a quarter of a million Romans and she knew the fallen charioteer had been trampled by the Blues.

'Which one was it?' she asked, without looking up. 'Which charioteer?'

'A charioteer named Cresces,' said her uncle grimly.

Flavia raised her head and turned to Jonathan in horror. 'Jonathan!' she hissed. 'Quickly! The curse-tablet!'

He fished in his belt-pouch and pulled it out.

'Read the names,' said Flavia. She felt sick. 'Read the names of the charioteers on that curse-tablet.'

'Castor,' read Jonathan, 'Cresces, Antilochus, Gegas, Phoenix, Tatianus and Eutychus.'

'Oh no!' cried Flavia. 'The first two charioteers mentioned have come to ruin. Do you realise what this means? The curse-tablet is working!'

SCROLL XIV

Cresces was dead.

Flavia pushed through the crowd of wailing stable boys and charioteers in the Pavilion of the Greens to see the figure on the stretcher. It was the handsome blue-eyed auriga who had driven her so cheerfully around the track the day before. His eyes were closed and he looked as if he were sleeping. Someone had removed his leather helmet and Flavia saw his glossy black curls. She hid her face in Nubia's shoulder and wept.

'He had a young wife and baby girl,' said a flat voice behind them.

Flavia raised her face to see Scopas standing behind them. His expression was inscrutable.

'Scopas!' A blond stable boy ran up. 'I still can't calm Merula! Can you try?'

'Who's Merula?' Flavia asked Nubia.

'Horse who goes berserk in first race,' answered Nubia, and whispered, 'That boy is groom who beats Scopas yesterday.'

'It is?' said Flavia. 'How can he ask for help after tormenting him?'

'Please help me, Scopas!' cried the blond.

Although his face was still swelling from his recent beating, Scopas did not hesitate. He turned and followed the blond groom towards the wooden stalls at the back of the pavilion. Flavia and her friends hurried after him. In a stall at the far end a black stallion was frothing and snorting, his eyes rolling.

'I've never seen him like this!' The blond stable boy was nearly in tears. 'I've tried everything.'

'Do not worry, Priscus. Scopas will calm him.'

The stallion was kicking the back of his stall and making the whole row tremble.

'Scopas! Don't go in there!' cried Flavia. 'Can't you see he's crazy?'

But Scopas was already in, and almost immediately the horse grew quiet. It's frothy flanks were still heaving and its eyes rolling, but it stood still.

After a few moments, Scopas bent, took a handful of yellow straw and began to wipe the sweat from the horse's quivering flank. He used firm sweeping motions and he spoke to the horse in Greek, his tone calm and matter-of-fact.

Flavia breathed a sigh of relief. The horse's eyes were no longer rolling and he stood more quietly.

'Priscus,' said Scopas over his shoulder. 'Come help.'

The blond stable boy nodded and hesitantly entered the stall. The stallion rolled his eyes at him and took two nervous steps back, then grew calm. Priscus picked up a handful of straw and began to wipe the sweat from Merula's other side. Flavia saw that the boy was weeping.

'Scopas, what's wrong with him?' asked Priscus.

'I do not know,' said Scopas, as he brushed. 'Horses are frightened by things that do not frighten most people. Perhaps a flicker in the corner of his eye frightened him. Or the scent of lion's dung or a hissing

122

sound like a snake. These things frighten horses. They frighten me, too,' he added.

'But would not the smell of lion's dung frighten all horses?' asked Nubia.

'This is correct.' Scopas blew softly into the horse's nostril, which seemed to calm him even more.

Priscus blew gently into Merula's other nostril.

'Something specific frightened that horse,' said Flavia. 'Something which didn't frighten any of the others.'

'Some horses have special fears,' said Scopas. Now he was using the flat of his hand to rub Merula. 'I know a horse in Delphi who was often whipped by a man wearing a yellow cloak. One day the man left, but every time my horse-friend saw a man in yellow he became wild with fear.'

'Maybe gadfly bites Merula on rump,' said Nubia.

'Or maybe someone fired a tiny poisoned dart,' suggested Jonathan.

'Examine him for puncture wounds!' called Flavia over the stall door.

'This is an excellent idea,' said Scopas. He and Priscus carefully examined Merula's sable coat as they stroked him.

'Don't forget his legs,' said Flavia.

'Yes.' Scopas began to unwind the strips of green linen from Merula's forelegs. Then he uttered an exclamation in Greek.

Flavia, Jonathan, Nubia and Lupus leaned further over the stall's half-door.

'Do you see it?' Scopas said, squatting back on his heels.

'No hair on his front legs!' said Flavia.

'And scars,' said Nubia, 'as if burned.'

'But those scars have healed,' said Jonathan. 'They look at least half a year old.'

'It happened a few months ago,' said Priscus. 'At the festival of Ceres. Merula went missing, and turned up a week later with burns on his forelegs.'

'Just like Sagitta!' gasped Flavia.

'Who took him?' asked Jonathan.

'We never knew,' said Priscus. 'He just turned up outside the stables one day. But I still got beaten for losing him.'

'He is calm now,' said Scopas. 'Cover him with a blanket and let him rest.'

'Thank you, Scopas.' Priscus hung his head and might have said something else, but Scopas was already closing the half-door of the stall behind him.

'I have to show you a thing,' he said to Flavia and her friends, and he removed an object from his belt-pouch.

Flavia examined the yellowish-brown object. It was about the size of her little finger, but twice as long. She sniffed it and then shrugged. 'It's beeswax,' she said, 'but I don't know what it's used for.'

'It looks like a lynchpin!' cried Jonathan, taking the object. 'But those are usually made of bronze. This is made of wax.'

Scopas gave a single nod. 'One of the sparsores found it on the track. He gave it to me.'

'Of course!' cried Flavia. 'A wax lynchpin! Just like Pelops used against Oenomaus in the myth. It's the oldest trick in the book!'

'Yes,' said Jonathan. 'The friction of the wheel makes it grow warm and then the wax melts, and the wheel comes off.' He frowned. 'But don't they examine all the chariots for sabotage?'

'Many times,' said Scopas.

'Someone is still trying to hurt the Greens!' said Flavia. 'And it must be someone who knows these horses very well.'

'Someone horses trust,' said Nubia.

'And someone who can come into the stables,' said Jonathan, 'without arousing suspicion.'

Scopas stood stiffly, his head turning from one to the other.

'Those all point to one thing,' said Flavia, 'a traitor among the Greens! This mystery is getting deeper!'

Lupus nodded his agreement.

'But why would someone do this bad thing?' asked Nubia. 'It hurts the horses.'

'Flavia,' said Jonathan, 'should we show Scopas what the beggar gave us?'

Flavia nodded. 'We have something to show you, too, Scopas.'

Jonathan handed the curse-tablet to him. 'What do you make of this?' he asked.

'I cannot read,' said Scopas, and handed it back.

'Even if you could read,' said Jonathan, 'you probably wouldn't be able to decipher it. It's in Aramaic.'

'Scopas,' said Flavia. 'Do you know any charioteers or stable boys who speak Aramaic.'

'Or who are from Judea?' added Jonathan. 'Most Jews speak Aramaic.'

'I do not know charioteers or stable boys who speak Aramaic,' said Scopas, 'but Urbanus is from Jerusalem in Judea.'

'I thought so,' said Jonathan.

'What does the tablet say?' asked Scopas.

'It's a curse-tablet,' said Flavia. 'It curses the Greens, and it names all four horses on the alpha team and also seven charioteers.'

Jonathan read out their names: 'Castor, Cresces, Antilochus, Gegas, Phoenix, Tatianus and Eutychus.'

'The first two have come to ruin,' said Flavia. 'Are the others all driving today, as well?'

'This is correct,' said Scopas. 'Most do not drive until after lunch. But Antilochus is in the race after next. I will not be able to help you now. Pegasus is no longer needed so I must take him back to the Stables of the Greens on the Campus Martius.'

'Then it's up to us to stop Antilochus from driving,' said Flavia as they watched Scopas go to Pegasus in his stall.

'How?' said Jonathan.

'Is Antilochus the Egyptian?' asked Flavia after a moment.

'Yes,' said Jonathan. 'He's the bald one with light-brown skin.'

'The one who worships dog-headed idol,' said Nubia.

Lupus mimed someone kissing Nubia's feet.

'Then I think I have an idea of how to stop him driving,' said Flavia. 'But Lupus will have to be a thief.'

Lupus had found a broom and was sweeping straw back and forth beneath the linen canopy of the Greens' pavilion. Wearing his wrist pass, and surrounded by so many other boys in green tunics, he was virtually invisible. Head down, he swept his way over to the portable shrine. Antilochus, the Egyptian auriga was kneeling before it, worshipping his dog-headed god. Presently Antilochus rose and made his way over to the refreshment table.

Kneeling before the shrine, Lupus pretended to worship too. Then, quick as a striking cobra, he took the dog-headed statuette and hid it under the skirt of his tunic. Sucking in his stomach, he was able to slip it under the place where the belt was tightest. Then he pushed his stomach out to hold the idol tight.

He stood, took up his broom and resumed sweeping the paving stones, moving gradually towards the curtain that sheltered the latrines from view. Just as he was about to go in, he noticed Urbanus standing beside an empty stall. The trainer was speaking to a greasy-haired man in a red tunic. They were too far away for Lupus to hear their words, but Urbanus's twitching whip showed he was upset.

A moment later, the man turned and hurried towards the bright exit of the pavilion, shaking his head. Urbanus looked around angrily, so Lupus hurried behind the curtain. If Urbanus knew where he was about to put Antilochus's god, he would be furious.

Flavia, Jonathan and Nubia got back to their seats just in time to see the Greens come last in the third race of the day.

'Achilles wasn't really trying!' Aulus was saying to his father. 'It was obvious he was only pretending to whip his horses.'

'What happened?' asked Flavia.

'If you'd been here,' said Aulus Junior acidly, 'you would have seen a Green charioteer not trying to win at all.'

'I think you're right, son,' said the Senator. 'Someone must have bribed Achilles to come last.'

'Probably someone from the Blues,' said Aulus.

'Though it might have been the Whites or Reds,' said his father.

'Is there any chance at all,' said Flavia carefully, 'that it could be someone from the Greens?'

'Don't be stupid.' Aulus Junior gave her a scathing look.

Flavia sat back on her cushion, and gazed down at the track. A smattering of applause had marked the entry into the arena of a group of Blue desultores.

'Sisyphus,' she said in a low voice, 'would someone ever want to hurt their own team?'

He gave her a keen look. 'Why do you ask? Do you suspect foul play?'

Flavia nodded. 'We think someone from the Greens might be trying to thwart their own horses and drivers.'

'Mecastor! Tell me more.'

'Someone did something to make Merula afraid—'

'Who's Merula?'

'The black stallion that bolted in the first race.'

'You think someone nobbled him?'

'What is nobble?' asked Nubia. 'Does that mean to tie legs together?' She and Jonathan had leaned over to hear.

'No,' said Sisyphus, 'that's hobble. Nobble means to tamper with a racehorse to prevent its winning. There are many ways of doing that.'

'Like using a wax lynchpin,' said Jonathan. 'Scopas found one in the chariot that lost its wheel.'

'Mecastor!' muttered Sisyphus again.

'We think it had to be someone from the Greens,' said Flavia, 'because a stranger would arouse suspicion.'

'I suppose the most likely reason to thwart your own faction,' said Sisyphus, 'would be if someone from another faction paid you a huge sum to throw the race.'

'What is throw the race?' asked Nubia.

'It means to lose on purpose. Or make your team-mate lose.'

'By nobble the horse?' asked Nubia.

'Exactly.'

'But why?' said Flavia.

'Money,' Sisyphus tapped the side of his nose. 'There are fortunes to be made on horse-racing. Remember I made eight thousand sesterces last September, betting on the horses Nubia fancied?'

They all nodded.

'Well, I'm not doing as well today,' he admitted, 'but if I had known that the Green chariot would bolt in the first race it would have improved my odds of winning. You can bet *against* factions as well as for them, you know.'

'Do many people gamble?' asked Nubia.

'Oh yes, many people gamble,' said Sisyphus. 'Some of them compulsively. Others have made their fortunes through gambling.'

The crowds were cheering as the troupe of Blue desultores left the track in preparation for the next race.

Jonathan leaned forward to be heard. 'My father says the odds are always against you and nobody can get rich by gambling.'

'He's right. The people who make fortunes through gambling never gamble themselves.'

'What do you mean?' said Flavia.

Sisyphus glanced around, then leaned in closer. 'There is a powerful patron,' he said, 'from the dregs of the Antonia clan. A few years ago he was a mere plebeian, the son of a butcher. Now he's one of the richest men in Rome. His name is Gaius Antonius Acutus.'

Flavia frowned. 'Where have I heard that name before?'

Sisyphus continued: 'They say he gained his wealth and power through men's addiction to gambling. He runs betting rings for large amounts at high stakes. When people get into debt from betting – which they invariably do – he loans them money at an outrageous interest rate. They try to win back the money they've borrowed, but of course they only lose more. Soon they're so deeply in debt that they've nothing left to sell or mortgage. At this point he makes them give him part of their business, or their house, or even their wives and children.'

'How can a man give away wives and children?' asked Nubia.

'Because a paterfamilias has absolute authority over his family.'

'Where does this Patron of Gambling live?' asked Flavia. 'Or where can I find him?'

'Trust me, my dear. You do *not* want to find Antonius Acutus.'

Flavia could hardly hear his reply because the crowds had begun to chant.

'Antilochus! Antilochus! Antilochus!'

'What's happened to Antilochus?' asked Flavia, jumping to her feet in alarm.

'He's not racing!' said Senator Cornix from the end of

the row. He had been speaking to Aulus Junior on his other side, and now he shouted to make himself heard. 'Apparently someone stole his god and he won't drive without it! The crowd is disappointed. He's one of their favourites.'

Lupus appeared a moment later, looking smug. He winked at Flavia. She gave him a beaming thumbs-up in return. 'Well done, Lupus,' she whispered into his ear. 'You've probably just saved Antilochus's life!'

A moment later, she turned away from Lupus and looked at Jonathan and Nubia. The crowd had stopped chanting the name of the charioteer who would not run. Now they were chanting the name of the charioteer who was going to take his place.

'Gegas!' shouted the crowd. 'Gegas! GEGAS!'

'Oh no!' cried Flavia, 'They've got Gegas to drive instead of Antilochus, but he's the fourth name on the curse-tablet! Our plan failed!'

SCROLL XV

Flavia stared at her friends in alarm.

'Gegas isn't supposed to drive until after lunch! But he's named on the tablet. He'll be killed!'

'Don't say such a thing!' hissed a woman in the row behind them. 'It's ill-omened.'

'We've got to stop him!' Flavia clutched Nubia's arm.

'Too late!' said Jonathan. 'They're off!'

Four quadrigae came cleanly out of the gates and stayed in their lanes until the chalk mark, then the Blues pulled smoothly ahead on the inside. The Whites and Reds came next, riding abreast and finally Gegas and his team of four dappled greys.

'He's conserving his strength,' said Jonathan, nodding wisely.

'Waiting until the other teams have spent themselves,' agreed Sisyphus.

'Then he'll come up on the outside for an easy win!' cried Senator Cornix.

'No,' said Nubia suddenly, and pointed. 'Look at bellies of horses. See how bloat they are?'

'Are they?' asked Flavia, peering at the horses.

'Yes,' said Nubia. 'Someone has given them very much water or food. The horses cannot run fastly with bloat stomachs.'

'By Hercules, she's right,' said Senator Cornix between clenched teeth. 'Even Castor couldn't lead those bloated creatures to victory.'

'There's still time to change my bet,' muttered Sisyphus, and hurried along the row towards the aisle.

'Pollux!' cursed Jonathan. 'That trick isn't anything to do with Antilochus. It's to do with the *horses*.' He glanced at Lupus. 'Looks like you stole his dog-headed idol for nothing.'

'At least it isn't a dangerous trick,' said Flavia, 'like a wax lynchpin or a crazed horse.'

BUT THE NEXT ONE MIGHT BE wrote Lupus on his tablet.

Jonathan nodded. 'Someone is out to get the Greens today, no doubt about it.'

'I've got to figure out who's doing this,' Flavia muttered fiercely, 'and why!'

'Flavia,' cried Sisyphus, returning in time for the last lap. 'Look across the race track at the seats opposite. Do you see the pulvinar? Now look below it and to the right. Do you see that stocky man in the red tunic and white toga? That's Antonius Acutus, the man I was just telling you about. The Patron of Gambling.'

'Mecastor!' breathed Jonathan. 'That's the thug who nearly bit my head off two days ago, while Aristo was changing money in the Circus Flaminius.'

Flavia shaded her eyes and looked across the arena. She had not seen the man before, so she tried to get a good look now. From this distance she could only tell that Acutus was a bear of a man – stout and dark – and with receding hair. About her father's age, she guessed: at least thirty-two or thirty-three. He was surrounded by an entourage of men in white togas over red tunics, no doubt his clients.

Lupus was tapping her arm and she looked down at him.

He was holding out his wax tablet and her eyes widened when she saw what he was writing there:

I JUST SAW ONE OF HIS MEN TALKING WITH URBANUS, Lupus wrote, AND THEY BOTH LOOKED ANGRY.

The Reds won the fourth race of the day. The Blues and Whites were close behind, but it was not until several minutes later that the waterlogged Greens staggered over the finishing line to a wave of booing.

As Lupus's troupe of Scythian desultores rode their ponies onto the race track, Senator Cornix hid his face in his hands. 'What humiliation,' he moaned. 'This is far worse than a naufragium. At least that way we go out in glory. Praise the gods Antilochus wasn't riding in that race. He vowed to fall on his sword if he ever came last.'

'Just as well you took his idol after all,' muttered Jonathan to Lupus.

'Come on!' hissed Flavia to her friends. 'I have a theory I need to discuss with you. I think I know what's happening.'

'For Jupiter's sake, girl! Stop coming and going!' Senator Cornix scowled up at the four of them as they squeezed past him.

'Sorry, Uncle Aulus, but I promised pater I'd buy him a souvenir,' lied Flavia, 'and I want to do it before the next race.'

'Oh, all right then. But I wish you'd sit still, like Aulus Junior.'

'So!' said Sisyphus a few moments later, as they stopped by one of the shops in the arcade on the outside of the Circus. 'What's our theory?'

'Sisyphus!' cried Flavia. 'What are you doing here?'

'Helping you solve the mystery!' He grinned. 'I have a clue.'

'What?'

'My betting agent just told me that someone's been placing huge bets against the Greens. Just like I said.'

'Who? Who's been placing huge bets against the Greens?'

'An old woman, probably acting for someone else. Here, come inside,' he said, as three men pushed past them. He led them through an arched doorway into a shop which sold the same sort of glass beakers as the stall in the Campus Martius. 'Does my information fit with your theory?'

'Yes,' said Flavia. 'We know that someone has been trying to ruin the Greens' chances of winning and we think the culprit works for the Greens.'

'An inside job,' said Sisyphus.

Flavia nodded. 'When you told me about the Patron of Gambling, I suddenly wondered if the motive could be money.' She lowered her voice. 'A short while ago Lupus saw one of Acutus's men arguing with Urbanus.'

Lupus held up his wax tablet: HE LOOKED LIKE MARS WITH GREASY HAIR

Flavia looked around at them grimly. 'Can you guess what I'm thinking?'

Jonathan nodded slowly. 'That Urbanus himself is indebted to Acutus.'

'Exactly,' said Flavia. 'It fits all the clues. Who knows the horses and drivers better than Urbanus? Who could easily replace a bronze lynchpin with a wax one under the pretence of checking the chariot?'

'What about Scopas?' said Jonathan. 'Doesn't anyone else think he's strange?'

'Scopas is strange,' said Nubia, 'but I like him.'

Lupus scowled and wrote on his tablet: HE IS FRIEND OF MY MOTHER. SHE ASKED US TO BE KIND TO HIM

'True,' mused Flavia, 'but Jonathan does have a point. Sagitta disappeared shortly after Scopas arrived at the Greens. Also, Scopas knows all the charioteers and horses and he could easily have replaced the lynchpin.'

'Oooh!' cried Sisyphus, rubbing his hands together with relish. 'It's exciting, isn't it? Is the culprit strange Scopas or enigmatic Urbanus?'

'I'm sure it's Urbanus,' decided Flavia. 'I know Scopas likes to be squashed by horses and that he's a bit strange, but after all, he's the one who showed us the wax lynchpin. Also, he can't read or write. And he doesn't know Aramaic.'

'But Urbanus probably does!' cried Jonathan.

'Exactly!' said Flavia. 'Who else could write a curse-tablet in Aramaic? Also,' she added, 'Urbanus knows where to hide things. That's probably why he got angry with you this morning, Nubia. You thwarted part of his plan by finding the sacred images. Urbanus knew if the images disappeared, his charioteers would drive badly. Or not at all.'

'That makes sense,' said Jonathan. He picked up a glass beaker and idly examined it.

Flavia looked at Nubia. 'Pegasus showed you where the amulets were hidden, but did he show you who did it?'

Nubia shook her head. 'Pegasus only shows me fuzzy image of man wearing hooded cloak,' she said. 'Maybe Urbanus, maybe not. Pegasus himself is not sure.'

'Extraordinary,' murmured Sisyphus. Then he frowned. 'But surely it's against Urbanus's interest to sabotage his own side. As head trainer, Urbanus gets a good percentage of the prize money for each of his winning horses.'

'Is it a lot?'

'Of course.'

'But what if he's deeply in debt, like those gamblers you told me about?' said Flavia. 'What if he needs to make lots and lots of money fast?'

Sisyphus nodded slowly. 'Yes. He could sabotage his own team, bet against them, and make a fortune. And because he's their trainer, nobody would ever suspect him.'

'Or what if he's not in debt,' said Jonathan, 'but just wants to become fabulously wealthy?'

'All those scenarios,' said Sisyphus, 'would make sense of the facts.'

'And they all point to Urbanus,' said Flavia.

'Wait,' said Jonathan, 'what if someone is bribing or blackmailing Urbanus, forcing him to sabotage his own team, but *they* are the person placing the bets?'

Behind the counter the shopkeeper cleared his throat. He was a cheerful-looking man in a grey tunic. 'Are you lot going to buy something or just stand there chatting all day?' he asked. 'There is a wine shop two arches down, you know.'

Flavia picked up a pale sea-green beaker from a table marked half price and took it to the counter and put down a denarius.

'Whichever theory you choose,' she said when she returned to her friends, 'Urbanus seems to be behind the sabotage. We've got to find out why, and we've got to stop him.' She turned to Lupus. 'Can you go back and spy on him?'

Lupus nodded and Jonathan patted him on the back.

'Be careful, Lupus!' called Flavia after him. 'We'll make an offering at the shrine for your safety.' She turned to the others. 'And we'd better make an offering for the charioteers named on the tablet. Until we solve this mystery, they're doomed.'

Lupus found Urbanus in the Pavilion of the Greens. The next race was about to start but the head trainer was standing beside a stall, with the hood of his cloak pulled up. He was rocking back and forth, as Jonathan's father did whenever he prayed. The trainer was repeating a phrase over and over under his breath.

Lupus crept closer and listened with ears as sharp as a rabbit's. Suddenly his eyes opened wide. Urbanus was speaking Hebrew, uttering a phrase that Lupus had heard many times before in the prayers of Jonathan and his family. But out of context, its meaning eluded him.

'*Selah lanu et hovoteynu. Selah lanu et hovoteynu,*' muttered Urbanus, using the guttural 'h' Jonathan called 'het'. Lupus could tell he was weeping.

'*Selah lanu et hovoteynu.*'

It was maddeningly familiar. If only he could remember what it meant.

'Where did you get the beaker?' said Aulus Junior, who had moved to sit between his father and Sisyphus.

'We've got some at home like that.' He spoke with his mouth full. Senator Cornix had just bought everyone spiced sausages from a vendor.

'I found it at one of the shops in the arcade,' said Flavia, and handed it to him. 'It's pretty, isn't it? I'm going to give it to pater.'

'Out of date,' said Aulus Junior, after giving it a quick glance. 'Two of the charioteers are from two years ago.'

'What do you mean?'

'See the names of the charioteers around the rim?' Aulus Junior gestured with his sausage.

'Oh!' She turned the beaker in her hand. It was made of pale green glass blown into a mould. 'I didn't even notice. It names Hierax, Antilochus, Olympus, and poor Cresces.'

'Hierax used to be one of the Greens' best drivers,' said her uncle, peeling back the cabbage-leaf wrapper from his sausage, 'but he was horribly maimed in an accident last year. Lost an arm and a leg, if I recall correctly. And Olympus rides for the Reds now. He's driving in the next race. Four teams of four,' he added.

'What's the name of the Green auriga in the next race?' asked Flavia.

'According to this programme—' Sisyphus rattled a sheet of papyrus '—his name is Musclosus.'

'Didn't Musclosus used to drive for the Reds?' said Aulus Junior to his father.

'I believe so,' said Senator Cornix. 'In fact, I believe they traded him for Olympus.'

'Olympus from my beaker is driving for the Reds now?' said Flavia.

'Yes,' said the senator and his son.

'Charioteers change factions?' asked Nubia. 'Are they not faithful to one colour?'

'Of course not,' said Aulus Junior, and rolled his eyes at his father.

'Charioteers are mostly slaves,' explained Senator Cornix, 'like gladiators. And – like gladiators – they get a percentage of any prize money. Some save up to buy their freedom, but that often takes a long time. Until then, they can be bought and sold on from faction to faction.'

'Don't you mind? When your favourite charioteer moves from one faction to another?'

'Of course we're sad,' said Senator Cornix. 'But that's life. Of course, it works the other way, too. Castor used to drive for the Whites. Then he was sold to the Greens three years ago. We were delighted about that.'

'Castor's a slave?' said Jonathan.

'Not any more,' said Senator Cornix. 'He bought his freedom last year, but couldn't bear not to race. He's stayed with the Greens of his own free will,' he added.

'Naturally,' said Aulus Junior.

'Would you still cheer him if he left the Greens?' asked Flavia.

'No,' said Senator Cornix patiently. 'We support colours, not horses or drivers.'

'But Castor would never leave the Greens,' said Aulus. 'The other factions are scum. Especially the Blues.' He took another bite of sausage. 'I hope you didn't pay full price for that beaker.'

Sisyphus leaned towards Flavia. 'Is Musclosus one of the names on the curse-tablet?' he whispered. 'I can't remember.'

Flavia shook her head. She put her half-eaten sausage

in the beaker and handed it to him so that she could take out her wax tablet. She had copied the names in the same order they were mentioned on the curse-tablet: *Castor, Cresces, Antilochus, Gegas, Phoenix, Tatianus and Eutychus.* She silently showed the tablet to them.

'If Musclosus isn't named,' murmured Jonathan, 'then maybe he'll win.'

'I don't think so,' said Flavia. 'If my theory is right, the Greens will lose every race they run.'

SCROLL XVI

'So much for your theory,' said Jonathan to Flavia, who was covering her eyes with her hands. 'No doubt about the fact that Musclosus just won the Greens their first victory of the day.'

'But at such a terrible cost,' muttered Senator Cornix.

Beside Jonathan, Sisyphus shook his head and tore his papyrus betting slip into tiny pieces.

The race had begun well, with the four teams vying for position and the Reds and Blues running neck and neck. Then, at the turning point of the final lap, the Reds' inside horse suddenly screamed and surged forward, pulling his team right under the hooves of the Blue team. Swerving violently around the terrible naufragium, the White auriga had to pull up his team to avoid colliding with the Shrine of Murcia, and lost all momentum. The track had been left wide open for the Greens chariot, which until now had been in last place. Musclosus carefully guided his team through the wreckage near the meta prima then flicked them up to speed with his reins. A few moments later they rounded the meta secunda alone and cantered across the finishing line to rapturous applause, the loudest Jonathan had heard so far.

Flavia and Nubia had both averted their eyes from

the naufragium, but Jonathan forced himself to look. Medics and sparsores were swarming over the carnage. The Red and Blue charioteers were both dead and three of the horses had to be put out of their agony. As the animals' bodies were being dragged off the track with hooks, Jonathan glanced across the track to the pulvinar where Titus was now sitting. After dropping the first mappa of the day, the Emperor had moved to the covered seating to join the idols of the gods and goddesses. Even from this distance Jonathan could see his grim expression. Only five races had been run, and already the toll was horrific. The track would have to be purified for the second time that morning and the programme was already running an hour late.

'Ill-omened,' muttered a woman behind them. 'These games are ill-omened.'

'Your theory about Urbanus must be wrong, too,' said Jonathan to Flavia. 'His faction won this time.'

'Jonathan's right,' said Sisyphus. 'It's also unlikely that Urbanus could have caused the crash of another faction.'

'Hey, Flavia!' called Aulus Junior. 'The Red charioteer who was killed was Olympus. That means two of the charioteers named on your beaker are dead and one is horribly maimed.'

'Maybe it is curse beaker,' said Nubia.

Flavia made the sign against evil. 'Don't say such a thing! That last crash was an accident.'

'That was no accident,' said Jonathan. 'The Reds' inside horse bolted exactly the same way Merula bolted. And at the same place – right before the meta.'

'This is correct,' said Nubia.

'But why?' muttered Flavia. 'Why?'

'I do not know why,' said Nubia slowly. 'But I think I know how.'

'Flavia, we have to tell Urbanus!' said Jonathan as they entered the Pavilion of the Greens. 'Otherwise, someone could die.'

'Like we told him about the curse-tablet?' said Flavia.

'This is different. This isn't superstition. This time we have facts. Nubia knows what frightened the horse.'

Flavia shook her head. 'I still think Urbanus is the culprit.'

'He couldn't have been the cause of that last disaster,' said Jonathan.

'Yes he could. I just have to find out how.'

'Here is the Lupus,' said Nubia.

'Lupus!' cried Flavia, as he ran up to them. She lowered her voice. 'Have you been watching Urbanus? Has he been acting suspiciously?'

Lupus nodded and glanced around. Urbanus was standing at the mouth of the tent, congratulating Musclosus, fresh from his victory lap. Lupus flipped open his wax tablet and showed it to them.

Jonathan read the tablet, then looked at Lupus. 'Urbanus was praying? In Hebrew?'

Lupus nodded and pulled them out of sight behind some stalls. Then he pointed to the place on his tablet where he had tried to write down the prayer using Latin letters. Although he had learned a little Hebrew living at Jonathan's house, he could not yet write the alphabet.

'Se lac la nu et co vo tey nu,' read Jonathan haltingly. Then his eyes grew wide. '*Selah lanu et hovoteynu?*'

Lupus nodded vigorously, then raised both eyebrows at Jonathan.

'Yes, Jonathan, what does it mean?' said Flavia.

'You should know that, Lupus,' said Jonathan. 'We say it every morning in our prayers. It means: *Forgive us our debts.*'

'I knew it!' cried Flavia. 'Urbanus is horribly in debt and has to sabotage his own team to win enough to pay back what he owes.'

'It doesn't mean that kind of debt, Flavia,' said Jonathan.

'It doesn't?'

'Well it *can*, I suppose, but usually "debts" means sins: *Forgive us our sins.*'

'Even better! That proves he's guilty.'

'What are you lot doing here?' said Urbanus behind them and Flavia jumped.

'Oh, you frightened us!'

'I told you four to get out!' said Urbanus, his dark eyes angry.

Flavia glanced at Jonathan. He nodded back firmly and she took a deep breath. 'Sir, we think we know why the horses are going berserk.'

'What are you talking about?'

'Tell him, Nubia.'

'When Merula runs past meta in first race,' said Nubia. 'I hear something on euripus.'

'What?' Urbanus scowled. 'What did you hear?'

'Something like very piercy flute trill,' said Nubia.

'And?'

'And then it comes again in race just now. Just before Red horse goes berserk.'

Flavia turned to Urbanus, 'Scopas told us that horses are sensitive to sound as well as smell. Could the shrill note of a flute drive a horse mad? Like fearful cavalry horses who bolt whenever they hear the trumpet?'

'Horses are having keen ears,' said Nubia.

'I know that,' snapped Urbanus. 'I've been working with them all my life.' He glared at Flavia. 'A shrill sound might irritate or spook a horse, but it wouldn't make him go berserk.'

'Maybe he is being trained to fear sound of flute,' said Nubia. 'Like horse who fears yellow.'

'That's right!' said Flavia.

'What are you girls babbling about?'

Flavia answered. 'Scopas told us about a horse who feared yellow because when he was little, a man in a yellow cloak had beaten him.'

'What if someone played a flute while they beat Merula?' said Jonathan.

'Then the horse would associate the sound of the flute with being beaten,' said Urbanus slowly. 'I suppose it could work. But what am I meant to do? Arrest every flute-player and whistle-blower in the hippodrome?'

'No,' said Nubia. 'But we can make piercy noise here.'

'Merula's not here,' said Urbanus. 'He's back at the stables.'

'We could see if any of your other horses react to the sound of a shrill flute,' explained Flavia, '*before* they get out on the course,'

'Don't you even want to know?' said Jonathan. 'It can't hurt and it might help. It might even save a charioteer's life.'

Urbanus narrowed his eyes at them. 'I don't see how

you can be right.' He stood back and gestured towards the stalls. 'But go ahead and try. Most of the horses running in the next few races are already here.'

Nubia pulled her flute out from beneath the neck of her tunic and blew the highest sound she could. Instantly there was a thunderous crashing beside them, as a stallion went wild in his stall. They all turned and stared in amazement.

'Master of the Universe,' breathed Urbanus, 'he was going to run in the first race after lunch.'

The horse kicking his stall and screaming in fear was Sagitta.

SCROLL XVII

'I knew it!' cried Jonathan. 'Finding Sagitta was too easy. Someone meant for us to find him. And right before the race, so there'd be no time to discover his new fear.'

Urbanus had sent a rider to the Campus Martius to bring Scopas. Meanwhile, he and Nubia were trying to calm Sagitta, who had knocked his groom unconscious and broken the arm of a stable boy.

'I think you're right, Jonathan,' murmured Flavia as she watched Urbanus and Nubia try to sooth the frenzied horse.

'Sagitta was like a Trojan horse,' added Jonathan, 'only filled with fear, not Greek soldiers.'

Flavia nodded. 'I've never seen a horse so terrified. Oh, Jonathan!' she gasped.

'What?'

'We've been so stupid. They don't *beat* the horse while they play the flute. They *burn* him!'

'The heartless scum!' muttered Jonathan.

Lupus nodded his agreement and angrily smacked his fist into his hand.

By the time Scopas galloped into the pavilion on a small bay stallion, Sagitta stood quietly, but his coat was drenched with sweat and his whole body still trembled.

'What is it?' asked Scopas, jumping off the horse.

'Sagitta went berserk,' said Urbanus, mopping his forehead with the sleeve of his tunic, 'just like Merula. They've both been trained to fear a flute.' He glanced at Flavia and nodded. 'Probably by association with fire, as you said. Luckily this African girl managed to calm him.' They all looked at Nubia, who was still speaking quietly to Sagitta and stroking his neck.

'We can't run Sagitta in the race,' continued Urbanus. 'If someone blows a flute or a whistle or even utters a high-pitched scream, he'll go berserk.'

'Couldn't you plug his ears with wax, like Odysseus and the sirens?' said Flavia.

'No,' said Urbanus. 'A horse would never run if you plugged his ears with wax. Besides, the poor creature is utterly exhausted from that outburst. Master of the Universe, I've never seen anything like it.'

Scopas looked up at Urbanus. 'Pegasus can take Sagitta's place in the alpha team.'

'He hasn't had enough training.'

'Glaucus gives Pegasus courage. They go well together. Let me drive,' said Scopas. 'Scopas does not understand people but Scopas understands horses. I will lead the alpha team to victory.'

'You've never won a race before,' said Urbanus.

'I won yesterday.'

'That was a slow practice run.'

'I won at Delphi. I won two palms.'

'This is Rome, boy, not the provinces,' said Urbanus with a scowl, but Flavia could tell his resolve was wavering.

'Three charioteers are now yellow,' said Scopas. 'I am very light. I will go fast. Please, sir.'

'What have you got to lose?' asked Flavia.

'Plenty,' muttered Urbanus. 'If the Greens lose many more races the dominus factionis will appoint another head trainer. I'll probably end up shovelling manure.' He turned to Scopas. 'All right, boy. But don't tell anyone what we plan to do. You'd better ride back to the Campus Martius and fetch Pegasus. The African girl can tie up his mane and tail while we're finding you a suit. The rest of you: Out!'

Flavia pulled Jonathan and Lupus out the wide door-way of the Greens' pavilion into the brilliant noonday sun. 'It's time for action,' she said. 'We can't just sit around waiting for the next disaster. We've got to try to anticipate what they'll do next.'

'What *who* will do next?' said Jonathan.

'Whoever's been sabotaging the horses, of course!' said Flavia. 'Whether they're in the Greens or not. Here's my plan. There's one more race, then lunch, then Pegasus runs with the alpha team. But the culprit still thinks Sagitta will be running.'

'Unless the culprit is Urbanus.'

'I don't think it's Urbanus any more,' said Flavia. 'He said Scopas could drive. That proves he's nice.'

'What? Letting a boy our age drive the fastest team in the most terrifying races ever invented?' Jonathan grinned. 'That definitely proves he's evil.'

'Assuming the culprit is not Urbanus, but someone else,' said Flavia, 'they'll be waiting to blow their flute when the alpha team runs after lunch because they think Sagitta will be running. Nubia thought the trill came from the euripus. That would make sense, because if someone blew a flute down there, the noise wouldn't be drowned out by the crowd and the horses would be sure to hear. Lupus, can you find a way to get out to the euripus and see if there's anyone out there? Pretend to be a sparsor or something? This is a method they've used twice. They might even try it again before lunch. Also, they might have another plan, in case the flute doesn't work.'

'Like what?' said Jonathan.

'They might sling stones at the horses or toss something in the chariot's path,' said Flavia.

Jonathan nodded. 'Or fire a tiny poisoned arrow,' he said.

Flavia looked at him. 'Jonathan, could you go to the curved end of the hippodrome and make sure there are no people with flutes lurking about? In case Nubia was mistaken and the sound came from the stands and not the euripus?'

'Of course.'

'Excellent.' Flavia looked around at them. 'Let's all meet back here after lunch, before the first race. By Pegasus's stall. We can compare notes and wish Scopas good fortune.'

'What about you?' said Jonathan. 'What are you going to investigate?'

'I'm going to spy on the Patron of Gambling. Gaius Antonius Acutus.'

Each faction had several sparsores standing at the outer edge of the track with ceramic jugs of water in wicker casings. Lupus shuddered as he remembered the fate of the brave red sparsor who had tried to stop Castor's runaway team.

The Pavilion of the Greens was full of jade light and

noisy chaos. Some horses were arriving from the stables in the Campus Martius, while those who had already run were being led back. Cartwrights were checking wheels, medics were examining charioteers and veterinarians were inspecting the horses due to run. Lupus followed two Green sparsores out of the tent. They went to fill their water jugs at the long fountain beneath a bronze statue of a bull. He waited until they had finished, then began to fill his own leather water-skin. He hoped nobody would notice that he was using a water-skin rather than a jug; he didn't have time to look for one now.

'Give me a drink?' said a voice. Lupus was surprised to see One-Leg swinging forward on his wooden crutches. 'I use my right hand for this crutch and without all my fingers it's hard to hold the cup with my left,' he explained.

Lupus grinned and mimed opening his mouth. When the beggar obliged Lupus directed a stream of water into the man's gap-toothed mouth.

'Thank you, young sir,' said the beggar at last, a dribble of water trickling down his thick black beard. 'Most kind.'

Lupus nodded. He had been a beggar for two years and he knew how humiliating it was to be ignored and despised. He gave One-Leg a wave and, as the trumpet blared and the starting gates flew open, he ran to the right hand arch of the hippodrome. The guard let him through and he emerged onto the vast space by the starting gates at the beginning of the track. Over to his left, a slave was going along the carceres and closing the double wooden gates. Up ahead the dust was settling to show a line of twelve bigae approaching the linea alba.

Lupus gripped his water-skin and ran towards the euripus. He could feel the heat of the sandy track through the leather soles of his sandals, for it was only a little past noon, and hot.

By the time he reached the central barrier, the lead chariots were already pounding back towards him, so he darted into the narrow space between the base of the near meta and the euripus. The sand trickling between his toes was cool here, because it was in the shade. He waited until all the chariots had safely completed their turn, then he cautiously emerged back onto the bright track.

Presently he found a niche in the marble veneer of the barrier wall and stairs leading to the top. He was up them in an instant and found himself on the wide smooth lip of a long rectangular basin filled with about four feet of water. The euripus of the Circus Maximus was made of five of these basins, built end to end. Some of the monuments were set between the basins and others rose directly from the water in them: the dolphin lap-counter for example. He tipped his head back to study it.

Seven gilded dolphins were set side by side on a lofty oak crossbar which rested on two columns of green marble. All but one of the dolphins had their noses in the air. Against the crossbar leaned a ladder, and a slave stood poised on the third rung from the top, ready to tip the second dolphin's nose down as soon as the lead chariot rounded the meta secunda. Lupus could see the slave's surprised face looking down at him.

He quickly knelt and pretended to fill his already-full water-skin. Then he stood and continued carefully along the top of the barrier wall. The lip of the basin was about a yard wide, big enough for him to edge past the painted marble statue of a discus thrower. Rising from the water ahead was a spiral pillar with a bronze statue of a woman on top. The wings sprouting from her back and the wreath in her hand showed that she was Victory. Beyond her, set between the second and third basin, was a two-storey hexagonal pavilion with a conical roof. Lupus guessed that the two men inside were judges or stewards of some kind. He didn't want to attract their attention, so he descended another set of narrow stairs to the track.

Back down here, on the right hand side of the track, he saw the foreshortened shadows of the barrier monuments sharp against the hot yellow sand. He was just passing through the coolness of the obelisk's stubby shadow when he felt the rumble of the chariots making their third circuit, so he pressed himself against the barrier wall. The roar of the spectators rose in volume as the field thundered towards him and Lupus saw why: a Blue biga and a Green were in the lead, and Blue on the outside was forcing Green closer and closer to the barrier wall.

If he didn't move, he would be trampled.

SCROLL XVIII

Lupus saw sparks fly as Green's metal wheel hub grazed the smooth marble veneer of the barrier. Along some parts of the euripus were niches for stairs. But not here. The chariots were almost upon him, and there was no escape.

Offering up a quick prayer, Lupus pointed the nozzle of his water-skin at the inside stallion of the Greens and squeezed. The horse was used to sprinkled drops of water, not a steady jet in his eye. He veered slightly away, passing inches from Lupus, who felt the blast of his hot breath and smelled his pungent horsey aroma.

The movement of the stallion had caused the Green chariot to veer into the Blue, which swerved to the right.

Lupus's tunic fluttered as ten more bigae rumbled past. No wonder most of the sparsores stood on the outside of the track: it was suicide to stand here.

But he was committed now, so when the rest of the field had passed – strung out now – he dropped his water-skin and sprinted along the base of the barrier. He ran across the freshly-marked white finish line and beneath more barrier monuments: a leaping lion, an altar and the egg lap-counter. Already he could feel the ground shaking as the lead horses came up behind him again. At last he reached the gap between the euripus and the base of the far meta and he dived to safety just as the chariots thundered past for the fourth time.

Gasping for breath, he sank to the cool sand and closed his eyes and offered up a prayer of thanks.

The strong smell of blood made him open his eyes again.

Where was it coming from? His heart thumping, Lupus stood and took a shaky step forward. The three cones of the meta stood on a stone base shaped like a crescent moon. Hidden in the shade of the base's inner curve – visible only to someone this close – was an open trap-door.

Making the sign against evil, Lupus took a deep breath and started down the steps.

It was easy for Flavia to find Gaius Antonius Acutus. But it was difficult to get close to him. He was surrounded by at least thirty of his clients. They were muscular, dark-haired youths, like the clients of another powerful patron she knew who often called his men 'soldiers'.

Breathing a prayer of thanks that she had left her green palla back at her seat and that she was wearing a neutral dove-grey tunic, Flavia slipped off her green wristband and put it in her belt-pouch. She was deep in the territory of the Reds here.

'May I sit here for a moment, domina?' she asked a round-faced matron under a crimson parasol. 'Just until I catch my breath?'

The woman smiled and nodded. Flavia perched on the end of the marble bench and pretended to watch the race. From here she was close enough to see Acutus out of the corner of her eye, and hear the raucous shouts coming from his entourage.

Acutus didn't seem to be doing anything suspicious, but from time to time she noticed that people would arrive at the perimeter of his territory and one of Acutus's men would take them off towards an arch. One thug in particular caught Flavia's attention. He was big and muscular, with greasy black hair and a belligerent face. He looked just like the statue of Mars in Ostia's forum. He must be the one Lupus had seen talking to Urbanus.

When a nervous-looking man with a heavy belt-pouch approached Acutus's group, Flavia saw the Patron of Gambling give Mars a nod, then turn back to watch the race. Mars took Belt-pouch by the elbow and guided him along the aisle. As the two of them began to mount the stairs towards one of the dark arches leading towards the shops, Flavia took a deep breath, rose from her seat and followed them.

Seven steps took Lupus down into a dim space reeking of blood. As his eyes adjusted to the darkness he saw an altar with the remains of an animal on it, perhaps a goat. Flies buzzed and he realised this was an underground shrine. The meat smelled fresh and he guessed the goat had been sacrificed early that morning. That explained the blood.

There was no cult statue here, but on the wall behind the altar was a fresco of Neptune flanked by rearing horses. The god of the sea held a trident in one hand and what appeared to be sheaves of wheat in the other. Lupus took a step forward to have a closer look, then froze.

Someone – or something – was hiding on the other side of the altar; he could hear breathing.

Without stopping to think, Lupus leaped forward.

A curly-haired boy darted out from behind the altar and Lupus saw that he was dressed as a sparsor of the Blues, with a blue tunic and headband.

And around his neck was a bone whistle.

Flavia followed Mars and Belt-pouch through the arch to a tunnel-like corridor where there were no shops or snack bars. Now she wished she had not left her palla on her seat beside Sisyphus; it was chilly here. From the arena came the sudden muffled roar of the crowd. The vaulted corridor was dimly lit by the diffused light of day filtering in. In the dank wall were shallow niches that smelt of urine. Flavia stepped into one of these as Mars turned to Belt-pouch.

She heard a deep voice: 'Have you got it?'

'Yes,' came the stammering reply.

The sound of coins chinking softly. 'That's not enough.'

'It's all I've got,' the second voice whimpered. It must be Belt-pouch. 'I've sold everything.'

'The Patron wants ten thousand. There's not half that here.'

'I'll get the rest to him by next week.'

'Not good enough,' said Mars. There was a pause and then Flavia heard a curious thumping sound, like Alma beating a carpet.

At first she wondered what it was. Then, when Belt-pouch began to gasp and beg for mercy, she knew. Her heart pounded and she pressed herself further into the shallow niche. Should she run or stay? If she ran, Mars might see her. If she waited until he came back this way, he would definitely see her.

Flavia stepped out of the niche, turned and ran.

Right into the arms of Gaius Antonius Acutus, the Patron of Gambling.

With a guttural cry, Lupus launched himself at the curly-haired boy. But the boy was already disappearing up the stairs. Lupus pursued up the steps into the arena. For a moment he was blinded by the dazzling afternoon light, but he could hear horses thundering around the meta, so he didn't risk moving out onto the track.

Then he saw a flash of something at the top of narrow steps.

There was a bronze ladder here: the boy had gone up onto the barrier wall.

Lupus scrambled after him, aware of the roaring of the crowd. Above him, a single egg of marble sat high on its pole. There was only one lap to go. Below him, the boy was wading neck deep through the water of the basin.

Lupus grinned and plunged into the water. Now he was in his element. He didn't need to walk. He knew how to swim.

The water was clear enough for him to see the boy's blue tunic and his brown legs pushing through the water. Lupus frog-kicked forward and his fingertips were just about to touch the boy's calf, when the boy's legs rose up out of the water: he had heaved himself onto the marble lip on the Palatine side of the euripus.

Lupus crouched down, then burst out of the water like a leaping dolphin and tackled the boy round his ankles.

'Oof!' cried the boy. The air was knocked out of him as he fell onto the wide lip of the basin.

Lupus quickly straddled the boy's waist and pinned his wrists to the slippery marble. Then he ripped the bone whistle from around the boy's neck and tossed it onto the sandy track below. In a moment it would be trampled to splinters by the horses' pounding hooves.

'Let go of me, you brat!' snarled the curly-haired boy and he tried to spit at Lupus.

'Ngheee!' cried Lupus, trying to say: Who?

'Ngeee!' mocked the boy. 'Ngee, ngee, ngee!'

Lupus shuffled forward so that his knees were pinning down the boy's arms, and he reached for his wax tablet. He would have to write his question. He hoped the boy could read.

Astonished by this strange behaviour, the boy stopped struggling and stared as Lupus began to write on his wax tablet: WHO DO YOU WORK

But suddenly Lupus was being pushed up and over, back into the water. He rose up spluttering and cursing, still clutching his stylus, just in time to see the boy jump down from the euripus wall.

Lupus was up after him in a second. There were no stairs here but it was not a long drop and the hot sandy track was relatively soft. The ground was vibrating and Lupus turned his head to see half a dozen chariots rounding the meta in a pack. This was their last lap, and the charioteers were whipping the horses that thundered towards them.

The curly-haired boy was only a few feet away, drops of water flying off his hair as he turned his head wildly this way and that. Then, ignoring the oncoming chariots, he started towards the stands on the far side of the track.

'Nnnngh!' Lupus tried to call out a warning as the boy ran out in front of a dozen horses.

A quarter of a million Romans rose to their feet as the boy in blue darted forward, then stopped to let a chariot thunder past and then ran forward again, darting, dodging, dancing. Lupus was just about to run after him when a cry resounded across the arena and Lupus stared in horror.

The curly-haired boy had tumbled under the hooves of the outside horse of a pair of the Whites.

SCROLL XIX

Jonathan had just reached the curved end of the hippodrome when a universal cry made him look towards the racecourse.

'That poor little boy!' cried a woman, and sobbed into her husband's shoulder. 'He'll be trampled to a paste.'

Jonathan's heart seemed to stop. Was it Lupus? The cloud of dust left in the horses' wake was settling but he could see no bloody smear on the sand.

'It's all right, dove,' said the man. 'He's all right. He survived!'

And now the dust had cleared enough for Jonathan to see a boy in blue limping into one of the arched entrances beneath the stands. Another boy in a tunic of the Greens ran after him. Lupus.

But now two guards were running towards Lupus from Jonathan's end of the arena. Jonathan could not hear their cries – for the crowd was cheering as a Red chariot crossed the finish line – but he could tell by the way they shook their fists that they were angry.

Lupus obviously saw the guards, too, for he hesitated, glanced at the arch under which the boy had disappeared, then turned and ran back towards the carceres.

Jonathan watched until Lupus disappeared through the arch. Only then did he allow himself a long sigh of relief. His friend was safe.

'Let me go!' cried Flavia Gemina. But although Acutus's fingers were plump and moist, his grip on her wrists was like iron.

'I don't think so,' chuckled Acutus. 'Not until you tell us what you're doing here.' He was balding, and his long eyelashes and heavy eyelids gave him the sleepy look of a bear roused from hibernation.

'Who's this?' said Mars, coming up to them. There was blood on the knuckles of his right hand and also on his tunic.

Flavia looked around desperately. There were a quarter of a million people at the races today. How could this corridor be so completely deserted? 'I was just looking for the latrine,' she lisped in her little-girl voice.

'No, you weren't,' drawled Acutus. 'I saw you spying on us earlier.' There was a dangerous gleam in his heavy-lidded eyes.

'I want pater!' wailed Flavia, trying to make the tears come.

'I've got a daughter your age,' said Acutus, 'and I can tell false tears.' He twisted her wrist hard and Flavia gasped in pain. 'See?' he said. 'Now *those* are real tears.'

'What shall we do with her, patron?' said Mars.

'Take her to Mamilia.' Acutus relaxed his grip on Flavia. 'This one should fetch an excellent price.'

'You can't!' gasped Flavia. 'I'm freeborn.' She was

about to show him her bulla when a voice behind her called out, 'Flavia! What are you doing here? The Emperor wants to see you at once.'

'Sisyphus!' cried Flavia.

'Excuse me, gentlemen!' Sisyphus stepped smartly forward and grasped Flavia's free hand. 'You're in big trouble, young lady! Keeping Titus waiting. Come on!' Acutus and Mars were staring wide-mouthed at Sisyphus's umbrella hat and did not protest as he pulled Flavia down the dim corridor.

She was expecting an iron grip on her shoulder at any moment but at last they emerged into the heat and brilliance of the September afternoon and the buzzing crowds of the hippodrome.

'Oh, Sisyphus!' sobbed Flavia. 'Praise Juno you found me!'

'Shhh!' he hissed. 'Keep walking and don't look back. They're following us. We're going to have to go straight up to the Emperor in the pulvinar.'

'Did Titus really summon me?'

'Of course not.'

'But he won't just see me unannounced!'

'You're right. He probably won't. But even if he doesn't, Acutus wouldn't abduct you from under Titus's nose. What were you thinking? I told you not to interfere!'

'I'm so sorry, Sisyphus. I just wanted to find out if Urbanus owed Acutus money.'

'How? By asking *Please, sir, does the Greens' head trainer owe you boatloads of money?*' Flavia giggled hysterically and Sisyphus shook his head.

'Here we are,' he said, as they reached the large

roofed box set into the stands of the arena. 'Let's hope he remembers you.' Sisyphus turned to the handsome Praetorian guard standing beside a marble column and said in his most imperious voice: 'Flavia Gemina to see the Emperor Titus Flavius Vespasianus, please.'

Lunchtime entertainment at the Circus Maximus was a hunt of hounds and hares down on the race track. Despite this diverting event, most Romans had gone to snack bars or baths outside the Circus to eat something more substantial than sausages wrapped in cabbage leaves. Some had assigned slaves to keep their places, others had left their seats empty, but a few had brought picnic lunches and ate these on the benches.

Jonathan mounted the hot wooden steps of the upper tiers, pretending to scan the rows for an imaginary friend. He was still listening for the sound of flute or whistle, but all he could hear was his own stomach growling. On the highest tier opposite the meta, he stopped to let his breath return to normal. He found a place in the cool shade beneath the roof of the colonnade, then leaned against a column, closed his eyes and let the murmur of the half-empty arena wash over him.

Suddenly he heard something which made him open his eyes and stand up straight. A man two rows down and to the right had just mentioned Urbanus. Jonathan leaned forward and rested his elbows on the wooden railing and pretended to watch the animal hunt. But all his concentration was focused on the couple below him: a man and a woman. They were sitting under a blue silk parasol which hid their faces from his view.

'No, it's true,' the man was saying. 'They say he and his family left Jerusalem ten years ago, when Titus was about to besiege it.'

'But I heard he wasn't married,' said the woman. 'My sister says he's one of the most eligible bachelors in Rome.'

'Eligible, perhaps, but he's still mourning his wife and children.'

'Ahh! A widower!'

'Yes. It's a tragic tale. He brought his wife and children out of Jerusalem with him, only to lose all four in the fire last February. He was out of the city, on business, but they all perished. Apparently,' added the man, 'the oldest boy was only fourteen. He wanted to be a chariot driver.'

'Oh, the poor man!' said the woman, and Jonathan saw her hand appear beyond the rim of her parasol as she made the sign against evil. 'Even so,' she added, 'perhaps my sister could comfort him after his loss.'

'I don't think she should get involved with him,' said the man. 'Urbanus may be rich and powerful, but don't forget: he's also a Jew.'

Jonathan found Flavia and Lupus waiting outside an empty stall.

'Where's Pegasus?' he asked. 'And Nubia?'

'We don't know,' said Flavia. 'A groom told us Pegasus was here a short time ago but we haven't seen him. We just got here. I was nearly captured by the Patron of Gambling,' she added.

Jonathan raised his eyebrows. 'What happened?'

Flavia gave them a quick account of her meeting

with Acutus. 'His men are brutes. If you can't pay what you owe, they beat you like a carpet! He caught me, but Sisyphus came to my rescue and while Acutus was watching he took me to see the Emperor. By the way, Titus sends his regards to you and your mother.'

'You saw the Emperor?' asked Jonathan.

Flavia nodded. 'Sisyphus and I went to see him and he granted me an audience.'

'Why did you go to see him?'

'To prove I have friends in high places so that Acutus won't sell me as a slave. Or something worse.' She shuddered. 'How about the two of you? Lupus, why are you damp?'

Lupus pointed out towards the euripus and gave a rueful shrug. He borrowed Flavia's tablet to write what had happened.

'An underground shrine?' she said, reading over his shoulder. 'That must be the one Urbanus mentioned, to the god called Consus. Why didn't I think of that? It's the perfect place to hide! And you think the boy with the whistle was one of the twin beggars who led us to Sagitta three days ago?'

Lupus nodded emphatically and wrote: WHAT IF THEY AREN'T REALLY BEGGARS?

'Great Juno's peacock, Lupus!' cried Flavia. 'You're right. What if those twin beggar-boys are the culprits? No, wait! What if they're working *for* the culprit? There are so many stable boys and sparsores around here. Put a boy in a faction colour and nobody would look twice.'

'It works for Lupus,' said Jonathan.

'It certainly does,' said Flavia, and thought for a moment. 'We still need to figure out who the culprit is. Who's giving them their orders. Did you discover anything, Jonathan? Any clues?'

'Not really. But I overheard some people talking about Urbanus. He's Jewish all right. He and his family escaped the siege of Jerusalem – just like my family – and they ended up here in Italia.' Jonathan stared down at his feet. 'But then last winter he lost them all in the fire. A wife and three children.'

'Oh Jonathan! How terrible.'

Jonathan nodded miserably.

'They must have been in the part of the stables that was burnt. Maybe that's why Urbanus was asking God's forgiveness,' she added. 'Maybe he blames himself for their deaths.' She glanced at Jonathan. 'People often blame themselves for things that aren't their fault.'

'Maybe.' Jonathan shrugged.

'Where is Pegasus?' said a boy's voice behind them.

Jonathan and his friends turned to see a young auriga.

'Scopas?' said Flavia. 'Is that you? You look so different wearing a helmet.'

The young Greek gave a nod, his hazel eyes bright beneath the leather visor. 'Where is Pegasus?' he said again.

'Isn't he with you?'

'No. I was getting dressed to race in the great Circus Maximus.'

'We just got here,' said Jonathan. 'We haven't seen Pegasus. Or Nubia.'

'But they are harnessing the other horses now,' said Scopas, looking into the empty stall. 'Nubia said she would bring Pegasus when he was ready.'

'They weren't by the carceres,' said Jonathan. 'Or outside the pavilion. And they're certainly not in here—'

'Jonathan!' cried Flavia, clutching his arm. 'What if the culprit's abducted them?'

SCROLL XX

'Excuse me, sir,' said Flavia to a guard near the entrance of the Greens' pavilion. 'Have you seen any horses leave here in the last hour?'

The guard grinned down at her. 'Dozens,' he said. 'I've seen dozens leaving on their way back to the Campus Martius. Seen dozens arriving, as well. What's the matter? Lost your horse?'

'He isn't lost. We think he's been abducted, and our friend, too!'

The guard's grin faded. 'Well, now, young miss. That's a serious accusation. You think I'd allow someone to steal a horse?'

'We're sure it wasn't your fault, sir,' said Jonathan quickly. 'We just want to find our friend Nubia. We think she was with Pegasus.'

'Pegasus?'

'The dark brown stallion with a flaxen mane and tail,' said Flavia.

'Oh, him! He left a short time ago.'

'Was a dark-skinned girl with him?' asked Flavia. 'About my age?'

'That's right,' said the guard. 'The girl who found Sagitta. She said she was taking him for a drink. But now you mention it—' he scratched his head '—I saw them taking him away. Back to the stables, I presume.'

'*They* were taking him back?' Flavia swallowed. 'How many of them were there?'

'Just the two of them.'

'Two men?'

'No.' The guard looked confused. 'The girl who found Sagitta and that one-legged beggar. He was with her.'

'One-Leg was with her?' Jonathan glanced at the others.

'That's right. That one-legged beggar who always hangs around here.'

'Oh, no,' breathed Flavia, 'What if the twins aren't the only ones pretending to be beggars? What if the one-legged man is pretending, too? What if he's really the culprit?' She turned to the boys in horror. 'And what if he's just abducted Pegasus and Nubia?!'

Nubia led her beloved Pegasus away from the Circus Maximus.

Half an hour before, she had plaited the last ribbon into his flaxen tail and had taken him for a drink at the fountain. The swifts shrieking overhead reminded her of the horrible naufragium earlier in the day, and she shuddered. She wished with all her heart that there was something she could do to stop Pegasus running the next race.

As if by magic, the one-legged beggar appeared. His beard and hair were clean and glossy, as if he had just come from the baths.

'Hello, sir.' She clapped her hands softly together and bent her knees in respect.

'That's a beautiful horse. He must be the pride of the stables.'

'Yes,' said Nubia miserably. 'He is now in alpha team.'

The beggar's eyes widened. 'This horse is going to race with the alpha team? That's a great honour.' He gave her a keen look, then said: 'You don't seem very happy about it.'

Nubia stared at him. None of the others had guessed her fears, but he knew. He *knew*!

'I wish Pegasus will not race,' she whispered. 'What if he falls and his legs crackle in the wheels and they must cut his throat and drag him off the track with hooks? I could not bear it!' She pressed her face against the stallion's neck to stifle a sob.

'Then why don't you do something noble?' said the beggar. 'Take him away from here and set him free.'

She turned her head to look at him. It was as if he had read her thoughts.

'Do you want me to help you?' he said, then added: 'Your kindness to me deserves a reward.'

Nubia took a deep breath, closed her eyes, and nodded. Her heart was pounding like a drum.

'Then here's what we'll do. I'll go talk to those two guards. When they turn their backs, quickly take the horse up the stairs of that little temple and right out the other side. Then go straight up the steep, paved street opposite. Once you round the bend, go slowly. I'll catch up. I know a place we can take him.'

And so here she was, leading a priceless racehorse up a hill away from the Forum Boarium. Her feet grew heavier and heavier, and a wave of nausea washed over her. Was she doing the right thing?

Two men coming down the road glanced curiously at her, but continued on their way.

A moment later the beggar appeared beside her, using his crutches to swing himself up the steep hill. 'Don't stop,' he gasped. 'Carry on. Quickly, before anybody asks us what we're doing.'

Nubia's heart thumped as they continued to climb. She listened for shouts or running footsteps coming from behind, but the only sound she heard was the steady clop of Pegasus's hooves on the paving stones and a baby crying from an upstairs window. The bright afternoon sun filtered through washing strung overhead and made the red plaster walls throw back a pinkish light.

'Where will we take him?' she asked, as they reached the top of the hill.

'To the Alban Hills, where he can run free,' said the beggar.

'The Alban Hills,' repeated Nubia. The name made her think of cool green pine forests and clear streams.

'We'll take him tonight.' The beggar mopped his forehead with a handkerchief.

'Can we not take him there now?'

'If we take him out of Rome in broad daylight, someone might recognise his quality. If we wait until after dark, nobody will notice him. Meanwhile, I know an empty townhouse just up ahead where we can keep him until it's safe to move him.'

'An empty townhouse?'

'Yes. Sometimes when a homeowner dies, his property is disputed by the relatives. None of them are allowed to live there until the case is settled. There's a house like that up here on the Aventine.' He chuckled.

'I'm just looking after it until the judge makes his ruling.'

Nubia nodded. So this was the Aventine, the hill that overlooked the Circus.

As if in confirmation, a trumpet blared off to her left, and she heard the roar of two hundred and fifty thousand voices. The next race had started. Without Pegasus.

Another wave of nausea washed over her. What was she doing? She had never stolen anything in her life and now she was abducting a priceless racehorse.

She stopped and crouched in the street and lowered her head between her knees, afraid for a moment that she was going to be sick. Presently it passed and she rose unsteadily to her feet.

'Don't worry, Nubia,' said the beggar kindly. 'You're doing the right thing. Horse racing's a cruel business.'

'You know my name?' she said.

'Of course.'

'What is your name?' she asked in a trembling voice.

'Hierax.'

'Hierax,' repeated Nubia, and nodded to herself. 'That means hawk.' She knew that Jupiter often took the form of a bird of prey. She also remembered the story of how Jupiter and Mercury had once disguised themselves as ragged travellers to test people. Only one old couple had shown kindness and the two gods had rewarded them.

Tonight Jupiter would reward her by taking Pegasus to the Alban Hills, where he could run free and graze on green grass and never again risk death in the hippodrome.

Tomorrow she would have to return to Flavia and

the others. What could she tell them? That Pegasus had run off. And that she had followed him for a long way before he finally eluded her.

The thought of lying to Flavia made her feel sick again.

But when Pegasus turned his head and snuffled softly in the hollow of her neck, she knew she was doing the right thing.

'Hierax?' said Jonathan. 'One-Leg's real name is Hierax?'

He and Flavia and Lupus had gone back to the Stables of the Greens to look for Nubia and Pegasus. But they had found no trace of them. Now they were speaking to the owner of the glass-beaker stall on the roadside.

'That's right,' said the stall-keeper. 'The beggar's name is Hierax.'

'And you're sure he's not one of the gods in disguise?' Jonathan looked pointedly at Flavia.

'No,' chuckled the stall-keeper, 'he's not a god, but he did used to be the next best thing.'

Jonathan's eyebrows went up in questioning surprise.

'He was a famous auriga,' said the shopkeeper. 'In Rome that's the next best thing to being a god. He was rich, handsome, followed by crowds of adoring girls . . . But then, two years ago he had a terrible accident in the hippodrome—'

'So that's how he lost his leg,' said Flavia.

'And some fingers and half the skin off his face.'

Jonathan nodded. 'And all his riches.'

'Now, that's what's strange,' said the beaker man.

'After the accident, his faction set him free and gave him his share of the winnings. He became even richer than before.'

'The one-legged beggar is rich?' said Flavia.

'Rich as Crassus.'

'Ohe!' said Jonathan. 'If he's so rich, then why does he dress in rags and beg for alms?'

Glass-beaker man shrugged. 'Don't ask me. I said he was strange. Who knows why these rich eccentrics do what they do? All I know is he may dress like a beggar, but he owns a villa in Baiae and a townhouse on the Aventine Hill.'

'How do you know that?'

'He told me. He sits here most mornings. Of course, he could be lying, but I know how much charioteers can earn, and he was one of the best.'

'If Hierax the beggar is rich,' said Flavia to the boys, 'then he can't be behind the sabotage or the kidnapping of Nubia and Pegasus. He has no motive.'

Jonathan nodded. 'I thought it seemed odd that a one-legged man could overpower Nubia and a big stallion.'

Lupus nodded in agreement.

'So if the one-legged beggar didn't abduct Nubia and Pegasus,' said Jonathan, 'then where are they?'

They were all quiet for a moment. Then Flavia turned to Jonathan and Lupus. 'Maybe Nubia took Pegasus!' she breathed. 'And she got the beggar to help her.'

'But why? Why would Nubia take Pegasus?'

'Because she loves him and doesn't want to see him hurt.'

'Great Juno's beard!' muttered Jonathan. 'You could be right.'

Lupus thought about it, then nodded, too.

'Oh, Nubia,' whispered Flavia, 'what have you done?'

'Behold!' breathed Nubia, as they passed through the double doors of a large townhouse. 'It is beautiful!' She stopped to look around the bright atrium. It was blessedly cool after the hot street.

Pegasus clopped across a honeycomb-pattern mosaic floor and bent his dark neck to drink from the impluvium.

Nubia laughed at the sight of her beautiful horse in the middle of this opulent house.

'He seems right at home here, doesn't he?' said Hierax, and swung forward on his crutches. 'Come into the inner garden.'

'Oh, it is so big!' Nubia gazed around the green garden with its apple trees and low box hedge. 'It is almost as big as the townhouse of Senator Cornix.'

'I hope there's nobody here!' said Hierax loudly. He used his good eye to wink at Nubia. 'My other beggar friends have found out about this place and sometimes they come to stay, too. The old woman might be here. Athena?' he called, then winked again. 'Look at that room.' He pointed with his chin.

Nubia's eyes widened. 'There is hay on the floor and a big trough of water and a manger.' She looked at him, awestruck. 'How did you know we would bring Pegasus here?'

He shrugged. 'I didn't. It's always been like this. The previous owners must have kept a horse here.'

Beside her, Pegasus snorted and she sensed his sudden disquiet. 'Do not be afraid, beautiful Pegasus,' she whispered, stroking the silky fringe of his pale gold mane. 'We are safe now. Don't you like this place? Come.' She led him into the room, with its sweet smell of hay and horse barley.

Pegasus went straight to the manger and bent his head to eat.

'No!' she cried. 'That food will be mould. That is bad for you.'

But she could sense the horse's pleasure as he ate. Puzzled, Nubia went to the manger, scooped up a handful of barley and sniffed it. 'It does not smell mould,' she said to Hierax. 'But it smells faintly wine.'

'Probably been soaked in it.' He gave her his gap-toothed grin. 'That must be why it's still edible. Speaking of food,' he said, 'I'm famished. How about you? Why don't we have some dates and cheese? We can eat them sitting on the upstairs balcony. You can see the whole Circus Maximus from up there.'

Nubia stared at him. This was like a dream: being led by a beggar into a palatial house with stables and a view of the Circus. Truly, he must be one of the gods.

'Great Jupiter's beard!' bellowed Senator Cornix, in a voice that turned every head in their section of the hippodrome. 'Where on earth have you children been? You told me you were going for lunch and it's nearly the fourth hour after noon! You are *not* to leave your seats until the races are over. Do you hear me?' Suddenly he stopped shouting and glared past Flavia. 'Where's Nubia?' he said. 'Why isn't she with you?'

'Oh, Uncle Aulus!' cried Flavia, and she burst into tears.

Sisyphus put his arm round Flavia and she sobbed into the shoulder of his leek-green tunic. She was dimly aware of a trumpet blasting and the roar of the crowd. Another race was underway.

'Tell us what's happened,' said Sisyphus.

Flavia raised her face. 'Nubia's gone.'

'Gone where?' said Sisyphus gently.

'We don't know. But we think she might have taken Pegasus with her.'

'She WHAT?' cried Senator Cornix.

Sisyphus shot his master a reproachful glance and said to Flavia, 'Why?'

'We think she took Pegasus away to save him from the dangers of the hippodrome,' said Flavia.

There were screams from the spectators as a Green chariot disintegrated on the track below them. Flavia glanced down at the carnage and then quickly away. 'Dangers like that,' she added in a small voice.

Sisyphus acknowledged this point with a wry look, then frowned. 'How did she get past the guards?'

'They know she found Sagitta and they didn't suspect her. We think she got the one-legged beggar to help her. He used to be a charioteer.'

'Who used to be a charioteer?' said Aulus.

Flavia ignored his question. 'Oh, Sisyphus! I'm so worried. Where could she have gone? What if she never comes back?' She blinked back fresh tears.

'There, there. Don't worry. I'm sure she'll come back.'

Flavia nodded and swallowed hard. 'What about Pegasus? Shall we tell Scopas? Or Urbanus?'

'Urbanus is not our biggest fan at the moment,' said Jonathan in a low voice.

'Then what should we do?'

'Nothing,' said Senator Cornix. His face was grim. 'If we report Nubia to the vigiles and they find her, then they'll probably execute her. Better wait and hope she returns the horse of her own accord. By Hercules!' he muttered. 'This is what happens when you give slaves, women and children too much freedom!' He glared at Flavia. 'When your father returns from Greece I'm going to Ostia to have a long talk with him.'

Flavia hung her head and nodded, too miserable to protest.

'Hey!' said Aulus Junior suddenly. 'Where's Lupus got to?'

SCROLL XXI

Lupus had spotted the curly-haired boy down on the track, this time dressed as a sparsor of the Whites. He knew it was the same boy he had chased, because of his limp. So while everyone was fussing over Flavia, Lupus slipped away and trotted down the marble stairs leading to the arena. He vaulted the bronze barrier and pressed himself close to the podium, so nobody on this side of the stands could see him. Then he sprinted to the little shrine on the track and slipped inside, passing from hot sun into the shady, myrtle-scented interior. He mouthed an apology to the marble statue of the goddess Murcia, who was very pretty. From here he could see most of this side of the racecourse including the curly-haired boy in white. He was watching the track stewards clear away the wreckage of a Green chariot.

Presently the Blues won the race. As the victorious chariot completed its lap of honour and came to a halt by the finishing box, Lupus saw the boy move away towards the carceres.

He waited until the prize and palm had been given, and as soon as the Blue chariot started back towards the exit, Lupus darted out of the shrine and ran towards the carceres arch.

When he finally emerged into the Forum Boarium,

he looked in vain for the boy in white. As usual, the area was crowded with horses, grooms and charioteers. He moved among them, searching here and there, and was just about to give up when he saw a curly head. The boy was limping past the noticeboard. Lupus dashed after him, weaving between people and leaping over piles of manure, and was just in time to see Limp mount the steps of the distinctive round temple of Hercules. The boy glanced furtively around and disappeared inside. Lupus crept as close as he dared, then hid behind one of the fluted stone columns.

Presently he was rewarded by the sight of Limp emerging again. This time he was dressed in the colours of the Greens.

Lupus moved round, keeping the column between him and the boy. He was close enough to see an ugly bruise on Limp's calf, where the horse's hoof must have struck him. Lupus followed the boy down the temple steps and back through the hot, busy forum to the Pavilion of the Greens. At the entrance, the boy waved his wrist at the bored guard, and entered.

Lupus dared not follow. Urbanus had probably worked out who had taken Pegasus, and he knew Lupus was Nubia's friend. The idea of being interrogated by an angry man with a whip did not appeal. Lupus sat in the shade of the bronze bull fountain and let the mist from the splashing water cool him.

The sun was two hands lower in the sky by the time the curly-haired boy emerged again, at the end of a line of horses being taken back to the Campus Martius. Limp was leading a bronze-coloured horse, and Lupus stifled a grunt as he recognised his favourite member of the Greens' alpha team: Latro! The boy was going more slowly than the others, letting the gap between Latro and the horse ahead grow wider. A crowd of joking charioteers walked in front of Lupus and when they passed the boy and the horse had vanished.

Lupus jumped up and looked around. He ran to where he had last seen them, and was just in time to see Latro's bronze-coloured rump disappearing between the columns of a small square temple. So that was how they got them out!

He followed Limp and Latro through the temple down four steps, then up a steep, stone-paved street of the Aventine Hill. He had to press himself into a doorway when the limping boy's twin suddenly appeared around a bend. No-limp was dressed in red, and as soon as he saw his brother they began to argue about something. Lupus peeked out of the doorway and watched as the limping boy pointed up the hill. His brother shook his head and pointed back down. Presently Limp won the argument; he and his brother led Latro further up the hill.

Lupus's heart was pounding. If he could follow them without being seen, they might lead him to the person they were working for: the person who was trying to sabotage the Greens.

Nubia and Jupiter-in-disguise sat on an upper balcony of the Aventine townhouse. From here they could see most of the Circus Maximus spread below them, framed by a lone umbrella pine on the left and two tall cypress trees on the right. Jupiter-disguised-as-Hierax had laid out dates and white goat's cheese on a circular brass tray which Nubia had carried up the stairs to the balcony. Jupiter had been nibbling all afternoon.

This surprised Nubia. She did not think the gods ate normal food.

She herself had no appetite. Guilt and anxiety made her stomach churn.

From up here the Circus Maximus looked like the Circus Minimus, and the crashes did not seem so terrible, though she still had to avert her eyes when a Green charioteer fell under the wheels of a quadriga. Jupiter-Hierax had watched the races with great enjoyment, often muttering, 'Yes, yes, excellent!' or 'Well done, boys!' He especially liked the crashes and he seemed to support the Blues.

The sinking afternoon sun bathed the spectators in the stands with a golden light. Soon it would be dusk. Soon they would take Pegasus to his Alban paradise.

Jupiter-Hierax popped a date into the left side of his mouth, which had more teeth than the right. A scar on his cheekbone moved up and down as he chewed. 'Tell me how you came to be here,' he said, as they watched little men clear up wreckage from the track below.

'Here?'

'Italia,' said Jupiter-Hierax. 'How did you come to be here in Italia?'

'Slave-traders burn my tents and kill my family.'

'Tell me,' said Jupiter-in-disguise, his eyes still fixed on the racecourse below.

Nubia hesitated. Was this another one of his tests? If so, she must be as honest as possible. 'It is more than one year ago,' she said, 'and it is night. I am in the desert with my family. The stars are so beautiful. We sit on the soft sand around fire. Taharqo plays his flute. He is my oldest brother. He plays the Song of the Maiden and the Song of the Lost Kid. Our goats are nearby asleep and I smell their goatness mixed with sandalwood which burns on fire.'

'Sounds nice.'

'Yes. I am happy. But I am also sad. The Song of the Lost Kid always makes me weep and so I am crying silent. My dog Nipur comes to lie beside me to bring comfort. He always knows when I am sad. I turn my head and I can see mother. She sits with my littlest sister Seyala in cloth sling. Seyala is fast asleep and my mother is rocking gently. Even my twin brothers Shabaqo and Shebitqo are quiet. When the last note of Taharqo's song dies, Father tells the story of The Traveller who visits the Lands of Blue, Red, White and Green.'

'Just like the chariot factions,' chuckled Jupiter-Hierax, stroking his dark beard.

'Oh,' said Nubia, gazing at him wide-eyed. 'This thought never visits me before.'

'Which is the best land?'

'The Land of Green,' said Nubia.

Jupiter-in-disguise snorted and took a piece of cheese.

Nubia looked out over the rooftops of Rome, now glowing red in the setting sun. 'That night the men come.'

'What men?'

'Men with long robes and twisty head wrappings and black veils like women. We run. Everywhere is screams and confusion. Mother cries "Run!" So I go hide behind dune with Shabaqo. I see the men attack Father. Later he lies very still in the sand and his dark blood makes a stain. Taharqo fights but they knock him on the head and chain him. They kill Nipur and other dogs, too. They chain my mother with some from our clan, some not from our clan. Then they set fire to tents. Mother is chained and cannot run, but now I hear screams inside tent.'

Nubia stopped and Jupiter-Hierax glanced at her. 'Who was in the tent?'

'I can not remember,' she said. 'But the men catch me then, as I stand outside tent, and they chain me to other women.'

'What happened to your family? The ones who survived?'

'All but Taharqo are dead.'

'How?'

'We march very long way. My feet were blister and my throat dry. On that journey many die and lie beside the road for jackals and vultures. My mother and baby sister fall beside road and they will not let me go to them. Now I have no more tears. We arrive at Alexandria, where everything is water and sky, and some people live in boats. They make us walk gangplank onto boat. Some of the girls do not want to go. They are confused. Then slave-dealer throws one in water. But her hands are still tied and she drowns. We scream and slave-dealer laughs.'

'Dear gods,' he muttered, through a mouthful of dates.

'You would think I do not want to live after all these things, but I want to live more than ever.' She turned to Jupiter-Hierax and added fiercely. 'And I want Pegasus to live, too!'

Fanning herself with a papyrus racing programme, Flavia listlessly watched the penultimate race of the day. She was hot and miserable and worried about Nubia. Senator Cornix and Aulus Junior were miserable, too, but for a different reason. During the whole day's racing, the Greens had only taken the palm twice.

'This is a disaster,' muttered Senator Cornix as the Greens finished in last place. 'That charioteer wasn't even trying. Someone obviously paid him off, like Achilles this morning. Come on. Let's go before the last race. Avoid the crowds.'

'What about Nubia?' said Flavia. 'And Lupus?'

'They had better be waiting for us at home.'

Flavia opened her mouth to protest, then thought better of it: Senator Cornix had a fierce scowl on his face.

'Make sure you take everything,' growled her uncle. 'Cloaks, programmes, umbrella hats . . . Flavia. What's that down there?'

'Oh,' said Flavia absently. 'It's just my souvenir chariot beaker.' She bent and picked up the beaker of green glass which she had put at the foot of the marble bench. Suddenly her skin seemed to grow cold.

'Hierax,' she said, staring at the beaker's rim.

'What?' said Sisyphus.

'What?' barked Senator Cornix.

'Hierax.' She looked up at them in horror. 'The one-legged beggar who used to be a famous charioteer.'

'That's right,' said Jonathan, adjusting his toga. 'The shopkeeper just told us.'

'He drove for the Greens.'

'Of course,' said Aulus Junior. 'That's why his name is on the green beaker.'

'He raced with the other charioteers named on this cup.'

'That's right. They were the top charioteers of the Greens,' said Aulus. 'Two years ago, that is.'

'What does it matter?' said Senator Cornix. 'Come on!'

'Wait! Stop! Don't you see?' cried Flavia. 'Not counting Hierax, two of the other three charioteers on this cup have died today. All except for Antilochus, who would have died if Lupus hadn't stopped him racing.'

'Antilochus wouldn't have died,' said Jonathan. 'Those waterlogged horses were going so slow that even I could have beaten them.'

'But his team came last!' cried Flavia. 'And remember what you said, Uncle Aulus? That Antilochus vowed to fall on his sword if he ever came last! Would he really have kept that vow?'

'Absolutely,' said the senator. 'Shame is worse than death.'

'I don't understand,' said Sisyphus. 'What are you saying?'

'If Antilochus had been in the race he was supposed to run, he would have come last and he would be dead, too! Because of his vow,' she added.

They all stared at her.

Her voice shook as she said: 'Someone's killing off the Greens from two years ago!'

There was a pause. Then Aulus Junior shook his head. 'What about Olympus? His team was sabotaged, but he was riding for the Reds.'

'Yes,' said Flavia, tapping the beaker. 'But his name is here. He *used* to ride for the Greens.'

'His name isn't on the curse-tablet,' said Jonathan, taking it out of his coin purse.

'Curse-tablet?' Senator Cornix and his son frowned at each other.

'That tablet is probably meant to scare the Greens,' said Flavia to Jonathan. 'It doesn't mention Olympus, because he doesn't race for them now. *But he did two years ago!*'

'Great Juno's peacock,' muttered Sisyphus. 'I think you're right. But why from two years ago?'

'Hierax!' cried Jonathan. 'His accident happened two years ago!'

'Exactly,' said Flavia. 'While driving for the Greens. He's the link!' She turned to the senator. 'Uncle Aulus, do you happen to know where Hierax is originally from? What country, I mean?'

The senator shook his head.

'I know,' said Aulus Junior. 'He comes from Judea. He's a Samaritan.'

Flavia turned back to Jonathan. 'What language do Samaritans speak?'

'Aramaic,' said Jonathan. He was staring at the curse-tablet. 'Samaritans speak Aramaic.'

'That proves it!' said Flavia, trying to keep her voice from shaking. 'Hierax himself wrote that curse-tablet, and then pretended to find it to panic the Greens. He knows Urbanus speaks Aramaic, and he knew we would give it to Urbanus. One-legged Hierax is behind this. I'm sure of it.'

'But, why?' they asked.

'I don't know why. All I know is that Nubia's with him and she probably thinks he's helping her. We've got to find her and warn her. We've got to tell her Hierax is not what he seems!'

As soon as he spotted the two lofty cypress trees rising above the red rooftops, Lupus knew where the twins were headed. They were going towards the place where they had found Sagitta three days before. They were taking Latro to the temple of Venus on the Aventine Hill.

Sure enough, a few moments later the twins passed through the columns of the portico and made for the little temple at the centre of the formal garden.

Lupus hid behind a neatly clipped box hedge and watched as they tethered the horse to a column. The twins were arguing again but presently No-limp went up a path to the right while Limp stayed beside the horse, scuffing the white gravel with his foot.

Lupus debated for a moment. Should he follow No-limp or stay with Limp? He crouched and ran behind the low hedge, then stopped and peered up the hill in the direction No-limp had gone. Above the red-tiled roof of the portico and between branches of trees he could see glimpses of opulent townhouses up on the top of the hill. Suddenly his gaze snapped back to a balcony just visible beyond the branches of an umbrella pine. Nubia was there! She was sitting next to the one-legged beggar. What was his name again? Hierax.

Lupus frowned. Flavia had said Hierax couldn't be behind the sabotage, because he was rich and therefore had no motive. But the twins had led him to the foot of this Aventine villa which must belong to Hierax. And that couldn't be a coincidence. Hierax had to be the culprit after all.

Should he try to warn Nubia? Or should he find Flavia and the others and get them to help?

If Hierax was rich as Crassus then he could afford to employ many people. There might be a dozen guards posted around the house.

Lupus grunted softly as he made his decision: he must tell Flavia and the others as soon as possible. He also had to save Latro from whatever torture Hierax and his boys might have in store. The obvious solution was to ride Latro back down to the Circus Maximus.

There was only one problem.

He could ride a saddled mule, and an unsaddled pony, but Lupus had never ridden a stallion bareback.

SCROLL XXII

The sun was setting and the pure blue bowl above Rome was filled with the piercing cries of swooping swifts. On the balcony of the Aventine townhouse, Nubia sipped her well-watered wine and watched a dozen tiny chariots burst out of the distant starting gates for the final race of the day. For the hundredth time that afternoon, she tried to see Senator Cornix's seats. But the two dark cypress trees always blocked her view.

'Those two trees look like trees in grove where we found Sagitta,' she said suddenly.

'They are,' said Jupiter-Hierax, topping up his goblet with wine. 'The temple precinct is right down there. I came across the missing horse that morning, on my way down to the Campus Martius. I tried to tell people,' he added, 'but you were the first to listen to me.'

Suddenly he stiffened and leaned over the balcony. 'By Hercules! What's he doing here?'

'Who?'

'Just a boy who steals my . . . um, apples. I'm going down to chase him off. Why don't you go check on Pegasus?'

'Yes,' said Nubia, putting down her cup and taking

the last few dates from the brass tray. 'I will check on Pegasus.'

Lupus tossed a stone so that it landed behind Limp. The curly-haired boy spun round to stare at the box hedge behind him, but did not leave his post.

Lupus cursed silently and lobbed another stone. This time the boy started towards the sound, then stopped and looked towards the path his twin had taken.

Lupus tossed the last and biggest stone. It made a satisfying crash as it struck the centre of a hedge near a bubbling fountain. This time the boy took the bait. With one last glance towards the house, he disappeared along the path leading to the fountain. As soon as he was out of sight, Lupus ran to Latro and untied his tether. But the horse's back seemed miles high. There was no way he could vault onto a stallion that big.

Thinking quickly, Lupus led the horse to the shortest in a row of plane trees, grunted for him to stay, then scrambled up the trunk. When he reached the lowest branch he swung himself out along it until he was dangling over Latro's back. But now he seemed miles *above* Latro, who was browsing on some thyme at the edge of the path and beginning to move away.

'Hey!' cried the limping twin, reappearing from behind the fountain. 'What are you doing over there?'

Lupus let go of the branch and dropped onto Latro's back.

Pegasus snorted a soft greeting into Nubia's ear. She fed him a date and stroked his beautiful arched neck. Presently she noticed that his tail was still balled up with ribbons and she started to untie them. It was getting dim in his room so she led him closer to the wide doorway, where the light was better.

She thought she heard the sound of the front door opening and voices, but when she cocked her head to listen, all was silent and peaceful.

'Your tail is tangled,' she said, as she removed the last ribbon, 'I must find a brush.'

She went to the wall where various pieces of horse tackle hung from pegs. She found a bridle, a saddle, strips of linen for the forelegs, a leather bucket for water, but no brush.

'Maybe it fell in the hay . . .' she murmured.

But there was nothing in the hay, only some smelly chunks of horse manure.

She rose and turned and saw a brush at the foot of the large bronze water trough. 'Oh, there it is.'

For a while she happily brushed his long tail. Presently she moved on to his mane, removing the green ribbons and brushing until it flowed like golden water over his dark neck.

Pegasus turned his head and gazed at her with his long-lashed black eyes.

'Oh, Pegasus!' Nubia spoke in her own language as she slipped her arms around his neck. 'If only I could keep you and take you home to Ostia. I could see you every day. I would brush you and feed you and we could ride on the beach and in the pine grove and over the salt flats . . .'

A sudden thought made her skin prickle. Leaving Pegasus, she went to the wall and bent down and groped in the hay. It was quite dark now but at last she found the chunk of horse manure she had seen earlier. She held it in her left hand and pressed it. As the outer crust broke she felt its moist inside. She sniffed it. This manure was fresh: not today's, but certainly from within the past week.

That could mean only one thing. A horse had been here recently. In this villa beside the grove of Venus. Could it have been Sagitta? Had the thieves brought him here, to this abandoned house where nobody would ever think of looking? They could have burned his forelegs with a torch while blowing a shrill flute and not a soul would have heard. Later, they could have taken him outside and tethered him to a column of the nearest temple.

And now her beloved Pegasus was here, in this possible place of torture.

'What have you got there?' said a voice from the doorway and Nubia started guiltily. It was Jupiter-Hierax, resting on his crutches and holding a flaming torch. He had put on a cloak and she saw with a thrill of horror that it was hooded.

Then her blood ran cold. How could she have been so blind?

Hierax was not Jupiter in disguise.

He was the culprit.

SCROLL XXIII

Nubia stared at the hooded figure in the doorway.

Now everything made sense. The fact that Hierax had known exactly where to find Sagitta. The fact that he had given them the curse-tablet. The fact that he had appeared just in time to help her steal Pegasus.

Something else occurred to her. Until recently this place had been inhabited. Perhaps the owner's body lay buried in the garden.

'Do we go to Alban Hills now?' she said, trying to make her voice bright and cheerful the way Flavia did whenever she was frightened.

'You know who I am, don't you?' he said.

'No?' she replied, in a small voice.

'Yes, you do. I can see it in your face.' He smiled, his eyes intelligent and cold above the dark beard. 'I can't allow anyone to stop me now. One more day like today and I will have destroyed the Greens.' He tossed a rope onto the hay in front of her. 'Sit down and tie your feet together.'

Nubia hesitated, her mind racing.

'Go on!' he said, swinging himself forward so that the flaming torch threw his distorted shadow on the wall behind.

Pegasus gave a small whinny of fear and backed into a corner of the room.

'He would have been an excellent subject for my training,' said Hierax, looking at Pegasus. 'He's already afraid of fire.' He pushed the torch further into the room and Nubia started back involuntarily. 'And so are you. Tie up your feet!'

Nubia sat on the hay and began to tie the rope around her ankles. 'Why?' she said. 'Why do you want to destroy Greens?'

'Revenge, of course!'

'What did Greens do?' Nubia fumbled with the rope.

'They destroyed me! I raced for them all my life, since I was a boy. I gave them everything. And what did they do for me?' He gestured down at his stump. 'This!'

'How?' said Nubia, trying to remember a trick knot Captain Geminus had once shown her, one that looked real but came apart when you tugged one end.

'My chariot,' said Hierax. 'Spun out of control. Before I could cut myself free of the reins my leg was caught in the spokes of another chariot. I was a mangled wreck.'

'Oh!' cried Nubia, her horror genuine.

He ignored her. 'They said it was my fault the chariot crashed. They accused me of using a whip on the other driver. So what if I did? Everyone does it. They said it was the judgement of the gods.' His voice rose a notch. 'How dare they? Look at me! Look what they did to me! Look what *he* did to me!'

'Who?' Nubia finished tying the knot and stood up.

'Urbanus. He was the one! I know the leg could have been saved. But he told the medic to amputate. Said it was necessary. The pain. I have never known such pain.

And then! Then they threw me out. Until that moment I was golden. I had wine, women, adulation. I had everything. Then, in one terrible afternoon I was abandoned and ruined. But I will have my revenge. And if I get rich taking it, then all the better!'

'I understand you are angry,' said Nubia. 'But please do not hurt Pegasus. Please let us go free. I vow I will not tell.'

'Oh, you'll tell! You'll go running to your little friends. That little mute boy is here, but my lads will take care of him.'

One-Leg was still breathing hard but he lowered his voice to a whisper now. 'After all the planning I've put into this – nearly two years' worth – I won't allow mere children to thwart me. Turn around. I'm going to tie your hands.'

Nubia nodded and swallowed. She had made a terrible error of judgement and she knew she had to make it right. Now was the moment.

As he reached to take a leather bridle from a hook beside the doorway she bent down and tugged at the end of the rope around her ankles. After a moment it came free, and she ran for the door.

Hierax looked up, his face frozen in an almost comical expression of surprise, then one crutch swung forward and caught her a fierce blow in the stomach. Nubia fell gasping onto the straw, unable even to cry out.

Suddenly Pegasus was behind her and over her, rearing on his hind feet and pawing at Hierax.

'Back, you brute!' Hierax thrust the flaming torch towards Pegasus, who writhed away, screaming. But the violent motion caused the one-legged man to totter and Nubia staggered to her feet just in time to see him fall back. The torch dropped in front of him and before she could do anything, flames blossomed from the hay.

'Master of the Universe!' cried Urbanus, when they finally found him back at the Stables of the Greens. 'I should have guessed Hierax was behind this. He's been threatening revenge for months.' He shook his head. 'And I thought you were behind the sabotage.'

'Us?' said Jonathan. 'You thought it was us?'

Urbanus nodded. 'You show up in Rome and find the missing horse within an hour, a horse that later turns out to be a terrible liability. Then lucky idols go missing, curse-tablets appear, a metal lynchpin is replaced with one of wax. All these things happened just after you came on the scene.'

'We thought it was you,' said Jonathan. 'I mean, Flavia thought it was you.'

'You thought it was Urbanus?' said Senator Cornix to Flavia.

Urbanus stared in disbelief. 'Why did you think *I* would do it?'

'Money, of course,' said Flavia. 'Lup— Somebody saw you speaking to one of Acutus's men.'

'Oh, that one!' Urbanus waved a dismissive hand. 'Just because he's the cousin of my brother-in-law, he always expects me to tell him which team I favour.'

'Anyway,' cried Flavia, 'we don't have time for that now! We have to find Nubia! She's in danger. Pegasus, too!'

Scopas appeared beside Urbanus, standing stiffly at attention. 'Nubia and Pegasus are in danger?'

They nodded.

'Zip q'nee,' he whispered to himself. 'Zip q'nee.'

Flavia turned back to Urbanus. 'Do you know where Hierax lives? Maybe we can find some clues about where they went.'

Urbanus shook his head. 'You know as much as I do. I detest that man. He was the cruellest charioteer I've ever worked with. He had no compassion for the animals.'

'Wait!' said Jonathan. 'The glass-beaker man told us that Hierax owns a townhouse somewhere on the Aventine Hill.'

'*Somewhere* on the Aventine?' cried Senator Cornix. 'Good gods, man! That's no good to us.'

'We've got to search the Aventine!' cried Flavia, blinking back tears. 'Which one is the Aventine, anyway?'

'It's the hill between the Circus Maximus and the river,' said Urbanus, 'by the Forum Boarium.'

'Then we've got to go there and ask people,' said Flavia. 'Maybe someone knows where he lives.'

'It won't be any use,' muttered Jonathan. 'There must be hundreds of houses on that hill. And it's almost dark.'

'Do you have a better plan?'

'No,' admitted Jonathan.

'Then let's go!' cried Urbanus.

Through the flames in the doorway, Nubia could see Hierax struggle to his feet, then lurch away on his crutches, an ominous figure in his hooded cloak. She couldn't be certain, but she thought she saw a curly-haired boy on the other side of the flames, gazing at her.

Something sparked a memory. Another face beyond the flames. A boy's face. A twin's face. Her brother, Shebitqo. He was the one who had been trapped in the burning tent that night in the desert.

'No,' whispered Nubia. 'No.'

The flames laughed and grew brighter.

Behind her Pegasus was screaming. She had never heard a horse scream like that before. The sound was almost human.

'No,' she said again, and she felt the strength drain from her and the world began to go dark.

Lupus whooped with terror as Latro thundered down the steep stone street of the twilit Aventine Hill.

Thankfully, they seemed to be going the right way. It was all Lupus could do to stay on board; there was no way he could guide the stallion. He cried out again as Latro took a skidding turn and he felt himself slipping. But he caught hold of the stallion's mane and hauled himself back up and gripped tightly with his thighs.

'Unnggh!' he tried to send Latro the mental command: Slow down!

The street was deserted, for it was almost dark now, but as Lupus reached the bottom of the hill he saw the distinctive silhouette of the circular temple of Hercules, black against the deep blue twilight. They were coming in to the Forum Boarium. Should he go left towards the stables or right to the pavilion by the Circus Maximus? If he made the wrong decision Nubia could die.

Latro was making for the bronze-bull fountain when a figure with a torch suddenly appeared before them, arms outstretched. It was Senator Cornix. The stallion reared and Lupus clutched the horse's mane. But Latro remained on his hind legs, pawing the air and whinny-ing in alarm as people shouted at him in different languages.

One of the voices was Flavia's, screaming for him to watch out, but it was too late. His fingers were slipping in the horse's mane and he knew with a terrible certainty that he was going to fall.

Jonathan watched helplessly as Lupus slipped off the rearing horse and fell towards the cold hard paving stones.

Fast as a whip-crack Urbanus was there and Lupus was safely in his arms. And here was Scopas, catching Latro's mane and calming him with soothing words.

As Urbanus set Lupus down, the boy uttered an inarticulate grunt, then pointed urgently back up the hill.

'You know where Nubia is?' cried Flavia.

Lupus nodded and imitated someone limping along on imaginary crutches.

'Hierax is with her?' cried Jonathan.

Lupus nodded vigorously.

'Then let's go,' cried Flavia, and Jonathan added, 'We don't have a moment to lose!'

Evil comes at dusk when the sun sets behind the city. It has the head of a lion, the body of a goat and a snake for a tail. From its mouth comes fire, a blast of hatred that ignites all before it. Now the hay is burning and the only way past the wall of fire is to ride through it. And this time she cannot wake up, for it is not a dream.

*

'No!' Nubia shook her head to clear it of darkness.

She could not let her beloved Pegasus die the way her little brother had died. She turned away from the wall of flames and looked around the room, lit bright by the fire. There! The trough of water. A few months ago she had seen men soak themselves and their horses in water and jump through flames unharmed. But at that time Pegasus had refused. He must do it this time. It was their only hope of survival.

She ran to the wall and took down the leather bucket and dipped it in the water and tossed it at him. The water drenched his head and mane but only seemed to make him more afraid.

'No, Pegasus!' she cried in her own language. 'We must soak ourselves in water and jump through. Or we will die!' She stopped for a moment, imagining she could hear screams from the past. 'No. Pegasus. It wasn't your fault and it wasn't mine. We couldn't save them because we were little. But now we are big. Now we must be brave.'

This seemed to calm Pegasus a little, for he stopped screaming. But she could see the whites of his eyes, still rolling with terror. Nubia sluiced him down again and again, making sure his tail was soaking wet. She sent him thoughts of vast cool water, of the Tyrrhenian Sea. But the flames were coming closer, the heat now almost unbearable, the smoke making her cough.

She quickly stepped into the bronze water trough. It was only half full now, but she was still able to submerge herself. The water was blood warm from the heat of the flames. She rose up dripping and wiped the water from her eyes and caught Pegasus's wet golden mane and pulled him closer to the trough. Then she stepped up onto its wet rim and from there onto his trembling back. He reared and pawed the air and she almost slipped off.

'No, Pegasus!' She clung to his neck and whispered into an ear pressed flat against his head. 'We must jump through flames. You can do it! On the other side is cool air and freedom. It was not your fault, Pegasus. Trust me. And fly, Pegasus. Fly!'

'It's on fire!' Flavia screamed. 'The house is on fire!'

Through the open double doors they could see a flickering orange glow and they could hear the roar of flames.

'The vigiles!' bellowed Senator Cornix. 'Sisyphus! Go find the vigiles!'

'Yes, master!' cried Sisyphus and disappeared into the night.

'Oh no!' cried Flavia. 'Nubia's terrified of fire. What if she's in there?'

'She's not!' wheezed Jonathan, and pointed. 'Look!'

They all gazed in astonishment as a girl on a horse emerged from the flames. The horse's hooves clattered on slippery paving stones and he almost slipped as he charged through the open doors of the townhouse and into the street.

Great orange billows rose up from horse and rider.

'They're on fire!' screamed Flavia. 'Quick! Put it out!'

'It's not fire!' cried Senator Cornix. 'It's just clouds of steam. Look. They're all right.'

Everyone ran forward. Scopas grasped Pegasus's mane to calm him as Senator Cornix lifted Nubia down from the horse's steaming back.

'Oh, Nubia!' cried Flavia, throwing her arms around her friend. 'Nubia, you're alive!'

For a long moment the girls embraced, while the others crowded round with congratulations and questions.

But presently the roar of the flames was too loud to ignore.

'Where's Urbanus?' cried Jonathan suddenly. 'He was here a moment ago.'

'I think I saw him go into the villa,' said Senator Cornix. 'He said something about other horses.'

'Nubia,' cried Flavia. 'Are there any horses still in there? Or any people?'

'No horses,' said Nubia. 'And I think no people.'

Jonathan cursed. 'I'll get him.'

'No, Jonathan!' cried Flavia. 'Wait for the vigiles. They'll be here any moment. I can hear their bells ringing.'

Jonathan shook off her arm.

The terrible fire he started last February had killed Urbanus's family. But now he could atone for that in a small way. He could save Urbanus.

Taking a deep breath, he plunged through the flaming doorway and dived straight into the shallow impluvium, rolling around to drench his clothes and hair. Then he stood up and shook himself off.

There was only one way to go from here, so he ran forward, into the garden courtyard.

A flaming timber fell in the spot he had occupied a moment before, but he did not allow himself the luxury of fear.

'Urbanus!' he cried. 'Where are you? Urbanus!' Then

a fit of coughing seized him. He remembered something his father had once said: *In a fire, more people are killed by smoke than by the flames.* Jonathan pulled his damp toga across his mouth and crouched down before running forward.

'Urbanus!' he cried again, and this time a weak cry brought his stinging eyes round to a figure lying at the opening of a room. The man was pinned to the ground by a fallen beam which had not yet caught fire.

Even as he moved forward, one of the doorways vomited a surge of flames and sparks.

Jonathan threw himself down on the marble pathway and felt the air sucked from his lungs. For a moment he gasped like a fish on the beach. Then the air returned. But only half a lung-full. The smoke was making his asthma worse. He knew a bad attack was inevitable. If he survived the fire.

With a superhuman effort, Jonathan raised the wooden beam a fraction and Urbanus was able to inch backwards until his leg was out from underneath.

'I think it's broken,' he gasped, his face white with pain. 'Leave me. Save yourself. I couldn't bear to have any more deaths on my conscience . . .'

'I'll help you . . . Come on.' Jonathan knew an asthma attack was coming. For the first time in many months he offered up a prayer: 'Please God . . . not until I get him out.'

Miraculously, he felt his chest loosen a little. He was able to stand and haul Urbanus to his feet and half pull, half drag the man beneath a burning apple tree towards the front of the house.

As they passed into the atrium, Jonathan realised Urbanus's cloak was on fire. He smothered the flames with his own wet toga, then pulled Urbanus through the double doors and into the waiting arms of his friends.

Then the asthma attack was upon him.

SCROLL XXV

'I think he'll be all right.'

Jonathan heard Hippiatros's Greek-accented voice and opened his eyes. He was lying on a narrow cot in a small torchlit room. 'Thank goodness you had the sense to tell me about the ephedron,' the medic was saying. 'If I hadn't given him that tincture . . . Oh, there you are. Welcome back.'

'Jonathan!' cried Flavia and he saw the faces of his friends as they bent over him. 'Oh Jonathan, you were so brave!'

Jonathan nodded. He felt exhausted but at least he could breathe.

'Jonathan,' said Flavia. 'The vigiles caught Hierax and the old woman, too. It turns out she was his mother. She made all the bets. But the twins got away. Apparently they used to be sparsores for the Greens. That's why they knew so much about horses and the Stables of the Greens.'

'Urbanus?' wheezed Jonathan. 'Is Urbanus . . . ?'

'Urbanus is going to be fine,' came Hippiatros's voice from nearby. Jonathan turned his head to see Urbanus lying on a cot next to him. 'His leg's broken but it's a clean break.' Hippiatros looked down at the head trainer. 'No riding horses for a month or two.'

Urbanus nodded weakly and smiled up at Scopas, who stood stiffly next to the doctor. Then Urbanus turned his pale face towards Jonathan. 'You risked your life to save me,' he said. 'Why?'

Jonathan shook his head weakly, then closed his eyes.

'I am sorry, master,' came Scopas's flat voice. 'You were kind to me. I should have saved you. I did not know you had gone into the burning house until Jonathan brought you out. I would have gone in after you. Even though I do not like yellow.'

'Don't worry, son,' said Urbanus. 'You were attending to Pegasus. And I know you would have risked your life to save me. You're a good boy.'

Jonathan opened his eyes in time to see Urbanus reach out and squeeze Scopas's hand.

The youth flinched but he did not pull his hand away.

Jonathan closed his eyes again, and smiled.

Nubia did not want to let Pegasus out of her sight, so Senator Cornix reluctantly gave permission for her to spend the night with the horse. 'Just don't tell anyone I allowed an unchaperoned girl of marriageable age to sleep in the Stables of the Greens,' he had muttered, giving her a quick pat on the head.

She and Scopas had eaten a bowl of mutton stew in the stable kitchens, and now they were bedded down on sawdust and hay in the spacious stall of Incitatus. Nubia lay wrapped in her leaf-green palla, wide awake in the warm, sweet-smelling darkness, close enough to Pegasus to hear his breathing.

'Nubia?' said Scopas. She could tell from the softness

of his voice that he was squeezed between Pegasus and the frescoed wall.

'Yes?'

'Flavia told me that Nubia is not your real name.'

'This is correct. Nubia is name slave-dealer gives me. It is name Romans give my country.'

'What is your real name?'

'Shepenwepet.'

'Shepenwepet. Do you want me to call you Shepenwepet?'

'No. Nubia is my new name for my new life with Flavia and Jonathan and Lupus.'

'Do you like them?'

'I love them,' said Nubia. 'They are my family now.'

'Yes,' said Scopas in his softly muffled voice. 'Sometimes it is possible to find a family not of your own flesh and blood.'

In the pause that followed Nubia heard Pegasus breathing slow and steady. She could smell his scent mixed with that of the sweet hay.

'Nubia?'

'Yes?'

'Why did you try to take Pegasus away from here?'

'I wanted him to run free in Alban Hills.'

'What are Alban Hills?'

'They are south of here. They are a paradise for horses.'

'Urbanus says the Greens have a stud farm in the Sabine Hills. He says it is a paradise for horses. He says Pegasus will be happy there because there are mares and green fields. In the summer he drives them up to the mountain pastures to toughen their hooves. Urbanus says the horses love that.'

'But I do not want his legs crackled in the wheels.'

'You think chariot racing is dangerous. You want to protect him.'

'Yes.'

'You are correct to think that chariot racing is dangerous. But it is also exciting. And some,' he added, 'were born to race.'

'What do you mean?'

'I cannot read or write,' said Scopas. 'I do not understand people very well. But I understand horses and I am an excellent auriga. I like to race.'

'I am glad you like to race. But I do not want to see Pegasus hurt.'

'Maybe Pegasus likes to race, too. Have you asked him?'

Nubia shook her head, even though she knew he couldn't see in the darkness.

'Why don't you ask him now?'

Nubia moved closer to Pegasus. The stallion sighed as she rested her cheek against his neck.

'Pegasus,' she whispered, 'do you want to race in the hippodrome or run free in green pastures? Tell me.'

He snorted softly and an image came immediately into her mind. Nubia gasped.

'Do you see something?'

'Yes.'

'What?'

'I see Pegasus with a palm branch in his chest strap. I hear the crowds cheering.' Nubia began to sob.

'Why are you crying?'

'He is happy.'

★

Nubia woke with the notes of a song playing in her head, and she realised she had not heard music in her mind for a long time. It was a song she knew. It was the song of a horse galloping free on a sandy beach under a golden sun and blue skies. It was the Song of Pegasus.

She smiled and stretched and turned her head to see her beloved Pegasus lying on the soft hay nearby. She smelled his aroma and felt his warmth and sensed his peace, and in that moment she was perfectly happy.

There was a lattice window high up in the frescoed stable and presently the sweet notes of a bird flowed through and she saw the sky growing light. Scopas stretched and yawned and turned his head to look at her.

'Zip q'nee,' he said softly.

'What does that mean?'

Scopas thought for a moment. 'When I was little, these words would run around my head like chariots in the circus. I do not know what they mean. But they comfort me. They are silvery-green. I like silvery-green.'

'Zip q'nee,' said Nubia thoughtfully, then nodded. 'Yes. They are silvery-green words.'

From somewhere inside the stables a wooden gong clattered, so they roused Pegasus.

Scopas showed Nubia how to mix a bucket of the best Cappadocian feed, a mixture of barley, beans and vetch bound together with the beaten yolks of sparrow eggs.

When they had fed and watered Pegasus they brushed him, working together in happy silence.

Nubia was plaiting the stallion's mane with green ribbons and Scopas was rubbing walnut oil into his hooves, when a noise at the doorway made them turn.

The blond groom called Priscus was standing with some of the stable boys.

'Salve, Scopas,' he said gruffly, and glanced at the other boys. They nodded their encouragement. 'We wanted you to have this.' Priscus stepped forward and held out a boar's tusk on a leather thong. 'It will bring you good luck for the race today.'

'Thank you,' said Scopas. He stood stiffly and allowed Priscus to slip the amulet over his head.

The other stable boys shuffled forward as more people entered the frescoed stall.

'Good morning, Nubia,' said Flavia, making her way to the front.

'Good morning,' grinned Jonathan, and Lupus waved.

'Good morning, Nubia. I hear you had quite an adventure while I was groaning in a shuttered room.'

'Aristo!' cried Nubia. 'How is your tooth?'

'The tooth-puller had to come again,' said Aristo, gingerly rubbing his jaw. 'But praise the gods: it's finally out.'

'And that's where I want the rest of you!' cried Urbanus cheerfully from the doorway. 'Out! You may have saved the day but I've got twenty-four races to oversee and no time to stand about chatting. Out, out, out!' He was leaning on crutches, but when Nubia started to pass he put out his hand. 'Not you, Nubia. You can stay. You're always welcome among the Greens. Here.' He removed his wristband and handed it to her. It was made of jade, with a tiny gold hinge and clasp. 'If anyone ever questions your right to be here,' he said, 'just show them that.'

Half an hour later, Nubia brought Pegasus to where Glaucus, Latro and Bubalo were waiting to be harnessed to the chariot, outside the Pavilion of the Greens in the Forum Boarium.

Scopas stood stiffly in his charioteer's helmet and pine-green leather jerkin. At thirteen he was the youngest auriga of all four factions, but she saw that he was perfectly calm.

Pegasus went eagerly into his harness and as Nubia helped adjust his chest-strap she sensed his excitement. She quickly slipped her arms around his neck. 'Dear Pegasus,' she whispered, 'as you glide above the clouds and beneath the stars, may the earth be your sky and may your feet be wings.'

SCROLL XXVI

The mappa fell, the trumpets blared, and twelve chariots flew out of the gates for the first race of the day.

'Alas!' cried Nubia. 'Scopas is very far away from the others.'

'He didn't get a good gate position,' said Jonathan. 'That's why he's in the far lane.'

'Oh no!' cried nine-year-old Hyacinth, who had been allowed to come with her twin brothers Quintus and Sextus. 'Scopas is in the far lane!'

'Scropus is in the far lane!' lisped the twins in unison; they were not quite six years old.

'Scopas, not Scropus,' snapped Aulus Junior. 'And he chose the outside gate on purpose.'

'I think you're right, son,' said Senator Cornix. 'He'll want to hang back at first, then come scorching up to win in the last lap and a half.'

'He'd better.' Sisyphus was biting his knuckles. 'I put all my winnings from yesterday on him.'

'Sisyphus, you fool!' laughed Senator Cornix. 'It's unheard of for a tiro to win on his first race in the Circus.'

'That must be why I got such good odds.'

'What odds did you get?'

'Two hundred to one,' said Sisyphus, with a quick glance at his master. 'If I win, I'll have almost enough to buy my freedom.'

The senator laughed. 'If that boy wins, I'll set you free this very day!'

'I hope you didn't place your bet with Acutus,' hissed Flavia.

'Of course I did,' said Sisyphus testily, adjusting his umbrella hat. 'Who else would accept such a large wager? He took my money personally and was extremely polite. I think our visit to Titus yesterday was an excellent idea.'

'Now he's in last place!' cried Hyacinth.

'Sporcus is last!' cried the twins. 'Sporcus is last!'

'I told you, you silly children,' said Aulus. 'He'll want to save himself for the final lap. And it's Scopas. SCOPAS.'

'Oh!' they all gasped as a White chariot took the meta too fast and ejected its charioteer.

'Euge!' they cried a moment later, as the White's horses came to an unsteady halt at the side of the track. The auriga staggered back to his chariot and drove slowly out of the arena.

'One down and eleven to go!' said Aulus Junior, rubbing his hands in delight.

'Oh!' they cried again. The Greens' alpha chariot had bounced in a deep wheel rut and for a moment Scopas was airborne.

'He's all right!' cried Aristo.

'There goes the fifth dolphin,' said Aulus Junior presently. 'He'd better make his move soon, he's still nearly half a length behind all the others.'

'I can't bear to look,' moaned Sisyphus. 'I think I'm going to be sick.'

'He hasn't even used his whip yet,' said the senator.

'That's right,' Hyacinth echoed. 'He hasn't even used his whip.'

'He's using it now!' laughed Aristo.

'They are quickening!' cried Nubia.

'Euge!' shouted Flavia. 'He's making his move. He's coming up fast. Sisyphus, look!'

'Sisyphus, look!' lisped the twins.

'Can't bear to.'

'Look, Sisyphus!' they all cried.

But the Greek was hiding his head in his hands and moaning, his umbrella hat tipped forward.

'Oh no! He's crashed!' cried Aristo.

Sisyphus yelped and raised his head.

'I made you look!' laughed Aristo.

Sisyphus glared at him and muttered something in Greek, then widened his kohl-rimmed eyes. 'Mecastor!' he yelped. 'He's in the lead! How did he do that?'

'He came up fast on the outside,' said Aulus Junior.

'He's not last any more,' added Hyacinth.

'Scopas may not understand people,' said Flavia, and everyone joined in, 'but Scopas understands horses!'

'Behold!' cried Nubia. 'Gegas and Phoenix are now using the pincer tactic to help Scopas.'

'That's right,' said Senator Cornix. 'They're blocking other chariots so that Scopas has a clear run!'

'But one of the Blues has got through,' wheezed Jonathan. 'The one with the silly winged helmet.'

'Hermes!' said Aulus. 'The Blue's star charioteer. And he's coming up fast.'

'Oh no!' screamed Flavia. 'Hermes is whipping Scopas!' They all rose to their feet and Lupus uttered a cry of rage.

'That's not fair!' gasped Jonathan. His knuckles were white on the bronze railing.

'He's bleeding!' cried Sisyphus. 'Scopas's cheek is bleeding. And he's slowing down. Oh, I can't bear to look.'

'Alas!' cried Nubia. 'Now Hermes is whipping Bubalo!'

'Why don't the stewards do something?' cried Flavia, close to tears.

'That stallion's not vexed,' said Aristo. 'Look how steady he is.'

'What a courageous horse,' said Senator Cornix. 'Go Bubalo!'

The crowds were booing Hermes but suddenly they erupted in cheers as his inside horse grazed the barrier and veered away, pulling the entire chariot off course towards the stands.

'He's out of the race!' exulted Aulus.

Lupus punched his fist into the air and Jonathan growled: 'Serves him right for cheating.'

'Here they come, around the meta secunda for the last time!' cried Aristo. 'It's the home stretch.'

'Here they come!'

'Look!' cried Jonathan. 'Now that Red charioteer with the broken nose is coming up fast.'

'Where did *he* come from?' yelped Flavia.

'It's Epaphroditus,' said Aulus. 'He always does that. Waits until the last moment and then comes from behind to win.'

'No! Don't say that!' moaned Sisyphus.

'Don't worry,' laughed Aristo. 'Scopas is still in the lead.'

'No he isn't!' wheezed Jonathan. 'Epaphroditus is overtaking him!'

'The alpha team must be exhausted!' cried Flavia.

'Scopas will get everything he can out of them,' said Senator Cornix.

'Look, the Reds are ahead!'

'No, the Greens.'

'Scopas!'

'Epaphroditus!'

'Come on, Scopas!' bellowed Sisyphus, and they all laughed.

'Come on, Scourpuss,' cried the twins.

'There's nothing between them!'

'I think he's going to do it!' wheezed Jonathan.

Hyacinth squealed: 'Look! That man is waving a green cloth!'

'Euge!' cried Nubia, 'Scopas is victor! Zip q'nee!'

But her cry was drowned out by the roar of a quarter of a million Romans.

'We won! We won!' Flavia and Nubia clutched each other's shoulders and jumped up and down. Lupus was giving his victory howl. Hyacinth was hugging her father and the twins were hanging off Aulus Junior's arms. Aristo and Jonathan laughed and slapped each other on the shoulders. Around them the spectators were going wild. Only Sisyphus stood in stunned silence.

'Unheard of!' cried Senator Cornix. 'For a charioteer to win on his first race. And driving a quadriga, too, rather than a biga. It's unheard of, I tell you.'

Sisyphus sank back onto his cushion and stared straight ahead. 'I'm rich,' he said. 'Fabulously rich.'

'And you're free!' said Senator Cornix, shaking his head and grinning. 'Congratulations, Aulus Caecilius Sisyphus. I hope you'll still work for me,' he added. 'You're the best secretary I've ever had and I'd be quite lost without you.'

'Zip q'nee!' cried Flavia, Nubia and Jonathan. 'Sisyphus is free!'

'Zip q'nee! Zip q'nee!' chanted the twins.

'Well done, friend,' laughed Aristo, and gave Sisyphus a hearty slap on the back.

'I'm free,' said Sisyphus, still dazed.

The crowds were cheering the alpha team horses and throwing gifts onto the sand: dates, chestnuts, scarves and even coins. Several sparsores of the Greens ran forward to gather the tribute.

'Glaucus! Latro! Bubalo! Pegasus!' cheered the people as Scopas continued around the racecourse in his victory lap: 'Yo, Pegasus!'

'Yo, Scopas!' cried Flavia.

'Yo, Scorpus!' yelled Quintus and Sextus.

Some people behind them took up the cry: 'Yo, Scorpus!' they shouted. 'Scorpus, yo!'

Soon the whole hippodrome was cheering: 'Yo, Scorpus!'

'Now look what you've done!' Aulus rolled his eyes at his little brothers. 'They're all calling him Scorpus.'

'I don't think he cares what they call him,' said Aristo, as Scopas rounded the meta at the far end of the arena.

The alpha chariot was alone on the course now; the

other chariots had peeled off through the arch at the far end of the racecourse.

'I'm rich,' murmured Sisyphus. 'And free.'

'Look at those horses,' sighed Flavia. 'They're so beautiful together. Bronze, grey, mahogany and nutmeg.' She exchanged a smile with Nubia.

'Why is Scorpus slowing down, pater?' asked the twins in unison.

'He's stopping to get his prize,' said Senator Cornix.

'I'm free!' murmured Sisyphus, still in a daze.

As a trumpeter played a brassy flourish, Scopas reined in his horses at the chalk finish line and jumped down from the chariot. He could not go far, for the reins were still lashed around his waist. The crowd's roar increased as a stocky man in a purple toga came down the stairs from the steward's box. He was carrying a palm branch in one hand and a leather bag and wreath in the other.

'It is the Titus!' cried Nubia.

'The Emperor himself is awarding the prize!' squealed Flavia.

'A palm branch,' said Hyacinth.

'For Victory,' said Jonathan.

'I'm free,' said Sisyphus.

'And he gets a bag full of gold, too,' said Aulus.

'And the victory wreath,' added Aristo.

'The Titus is placing it on his head,' said Nubia.

As Titus started back up the stairs to the finishing box, they all saw Scopas turn and wave at them.

'Wave to Scopas, everybody!' said Flavia. 'He's waving at us.'

'No,' said Jonathan, 'he's waving at Nubia!'

'Jonathan's right, Nubia,' said Aristo. 'He's beckoning you! Go to him.'

'She can't go down on the track,' protested Aulus Junior. 'Spectators aren't allowed down there.'

'I've never heard of a charioteer winning the palm on his first race, either,' said Senator Cornix. 'I think it's a day for new precedents. Go on, Nubia,' he said. 'I command it!'

'But . . .'

'Go to him!' they all cried.

'Euge!' Sisyphus leapt to his feet and tossed his umbrella hat onto the racecourse and yelled: 'I'm free!'

Nubia laughed and got up from her seat and edged along the front row and ran down the steps and clambered over the bronze barrier and out onto the sandy track, still cool in the shade of morning. The roar of the crowds increased as she reached Scopas in his chariot.

'You won!' she cried.

'Yes, I won.' He handed her the palm branch. 'This is your victory, too,' he said. 'Pegasus ran well before, but this time he was full of red.'

'He was full of red?'

'Full of courage. Climb up behind me.'

Nubia stepped up on to the springy floor of the chariot and hooked her left arm firmly around his waist. Scopas stiffened slightly and she remembered he did not like to be touched. But there was nothing else to hold on to and he did not protest.

Nubia held the palm branch in her right hand. It was surprisingly heavy and it rattled as the chariot turned under the flick of Scopas's reins. The four horses were now pulling the chariot slowly back towards the carceres. The pleasant odour of horse's sweat and leather and cool sand filled her head and made her spirit soar.

'Hold up the branch,' he said, over his shoulder.

Nubia did so, and the crowd went wild.

'Scorpus! Scorpus! SCORPUS!'

'They are cheering you,' said Nubia in Scopas's ear. 'But they are calling you Scorpus not Scopas.'

He shrugged.

'Does it not bother you?'

'No,' he said, over his shoulder. 'I do not mind. Scorpus can be my new name for my new life.'

Nubia laughed.

'Look at Pegasus,' he said, and she could barely hear him above the roar of the crowds. 'See how he holds his head? He knows how well he did. And he knows the crowds are cheering him. Do you see?'

'Yes. I see.'

'Jump off.'

'What?'

'Jump off the back. Give Pegasus the palm branch. I promised him he could have it.'

Nubia let go of Scopas and stepped back and down onto the track.

The chariot was moving at a walking pace and she easily caught up to Pegasus. He nodded his head and looked at her from under his golden forelock, the only part of his mane not tied in ribbons.

'Here, beautiful Pegasus,' said Nubia walking backwards before him. 'This is for you. You helped win the race and you overcame your fear!' She slipped the palm branch between the fleecy chest strap of his harness and his muscular chest.

Pegasus tossed his dark head proudly and the crowd roared its approval. Nubia moved back to walk beside white-socked Bubalo and she found she was laughing and crying at the same time.

As they approached the exit of the hippodrome Nubia looked at Pegasus. 'Oh, Pegasus,' she whispered in her own language. 'I love you so much, and I wish we could be together. But I can see that this is where you belong.' Then she smiled at all four beautiful horses. 'I am so proud of you all,' she said. 'Latro, Glaucus, Bubalo and dear Pegasus. If life is a circus, then today you are its greatest heroes.'

FINIS

ARISTO'S SCROLL

adoratio (ad-or-*ah*-tee-oh)
the act of worshipping a god or goddess
Aeneas (uh-*nee*-ass)
Trojan hero who fled his burning city and eventually
settled in Italia, becoming the father of the Roman race
Aesculapius (eye-*skew*-lape-ee-uss)
god of healing; his temple was on the Tiber Island near
the Forum Boarium
Alban Hills
hills southeast of Rome, reached by the famous Appian
Way
albati (all-*bah*-tee)
Latin for 'Whites', i.e. the White Faction
amphitheatre (*am*-fee-theatre)
an oval-shaped stadium for watching gladiator shows,
beast fights and the execution of criminals
Ara Maxima (*ah*-rah *max*-im-uh)
ancient altar to Hercules in the Forum Boarium (Cattle
Market) near the starting-gates of the Circus Maximus
Athena (ath-*ee*-nuh)
Greek goddess of wisdom, war, the arts, literature,
philosophy and women's handicraft; her Roman
equivalent is Minerva

atrium (*eh*-tree-um)

the reception room in larger Roman homes, often with skylight and pool

aureus (*oh*-ray-uss)

small gold coin worth one hundred sesterces

auriga (oh-*ree*-ga)

Latin for 'charioteer'; like gladiators, most were slaves or freedmen

Aventine (*av*-en-tine)

one of Rome's seven hills, it lies between the Tiber and the western side of the Circus Maximus

Baiae (*bye*-eye)

spa town – and residence of rich Romans – on the Bay of Naples (modern Baia)

Bellerophon (bel-*air*-oh-fon)

mythical hero who tamed the winged horse Pegasus and killed the Chimera

biga (*big*-uh)

a chariot pulled by two horses, more than one are bigae (*big*-eye)

Britannicus (bri-*tan*-ick-uss)

friend of Titus, son and heir of the Emperor Claudius, possibly was poisoned by Nero

bulla (bull-uh)

charm or amulet worn by all freeborn boys and many freeborn girls

Caligula (ka-*lig*-yoo-la)

Emperor who ruled from AD 37–41; he was a keen supporter of the Greens

Campus Martius (*kam*-puss *marsh*-yuss)

flat area in a bend of the Tiber northwest of the Circus

Maximus; near the modern Campo dei Fiori; each of the
four chariot racing factions had stables there

Capitoline (*kap*-it-oh-line)
Roman hill with the great Temple of Jupiter at its top; the
terrible fire of the winter of AD 80 probably started there

Cappadocia (kap-a-*dosh*-uh)
country in Asia Minor (modern Turkey) which was
famous for breeding horses

captain
right-hand yoke horse, arguably the most important
position in a four-horse team

carceres (*kar*-ker-raze)
Latin for 'cells'; the starting gates for horses in a race,
designed to spring open simultaneously

Castor (*kas*-tor)
one of the famous twins of Greek mythology (Pollux
being the other)

centaur (*sen*-tar)
mythological creature with the torso and head of a
human, but the body and legs of a horse

Ceres (see-reez)
goddess of agriculture and grain, the final day of her
festival in April, the Cerialia, was celebrated with chariot
races in the Circus Maximus

chariot (chair-*ee*-ot)
a low vehicle on two wheels pulled by two or more
horses and with a standing driver; racing chariots were
quite different from heavy ceremonial chariots: they were
small and light and therefore very fast

chimera (kime-*air*-uh)
> mythical fire-breathing monster with lion's head, goat's body and serpent's tail

circus (*sir*-kuss)
> although the Latin word 'circus' means 'circle', ancient racecourses for equestrian events were long, thin ovals rather than circles; the simplest comprised a starting line, turning post and finishing line; the most elaborate had stands, starting gates, arches, monuments, temples and towers for stewards to observe the races

Circus Flaminius (*sir*-kuss fluh-*min*-ee-uss)
> racecourse and market place opposite the Tiber Island near the Theatre of Marcellus and the faction stables, it was at the southern end of the Campus Martius

Circus Maximus (*sir*-kuss *max*-im-uss)
> the greatest racecourse in the Roman world, in the valley between the Palatine and Aventine Hills in Rome; most of our knowledge about it comes from literary sources and depictions on cups, lamps, mosaics and reliefs

Clivus Publicius (*klee*-vuss poo-*blik*-ee-uss)
> one of the oldest paved roads in Rome, on the Aventine Hill

Clivus Scauri (*klee*-vuss *scow*-ree)
> modern Clivo di Scouri; a steep road on the Caelian Hill near the Circus Maximus

colonnade (kal-uh-*nayd*)
> covered walkway lined with columns at regular intervals

Consus (*kon*-suss)
> ancient deity of harvest storehouses, with an underground altar near the southern turning post in the Circus Maximus; he became associated with Neptune

Crassus (*krass*-uss)

Marcus Licinius Crassus was a friend of Julius Caesar and so wealthy that he earned the nickname 'Dives' (Rich)

denarius (den-*are*-ee-us)

small silver coin worth four sesterces

desultores (day-sul-*tore*-raze)

acrobats who leapt from one horse to the other, they probably performed between races

domina (*dom*-in-ah)

Latin word which means 'mistress'; a polite form of address for a woman

dominus factionis (*doh*-mee-noose fak-tee-*oh*-niss)

master of a faction; at the time this story takes place, most factions were owned by rich men of the equestrian class

Domitian (duh-*mish*-un)

son of Vespasian and younger brother to the Emperor Titus

ephedron (*eff*-ed-ron)

herb mentioned by Pliny the Elder and still used today in the treatment of asthma

euge! (*oh*-gay)

Latin exclamation: 'hurray!'

euripus (yur-*ee*-puss)

Latin for 'channel'; the water-filled central barrier of the Circus Maximus

factio (*fak*-tee-oh)

Latin for 'party' or 'team'; in chariot racing each faction had its own owners, trainers, grooms, medics, veterinarians, carpenters, charioteers and horses; at the time of this story there were four factions: Reds, Whites, Blues and Greens

fasti (*fas*-tee)

calendar marking holidays and business days; also the name of a book of poetry about Roman festivals by the poet Ovid

Felix (*fee*-licks)

Pollius Felix was a rich patron and poet who lived near Surrentum

Flavia (*flay*-vee-a)

a name, meaning 'fair-haired'; Flavius is the masculine form of this name

forum (*for*-um)

ancient marketplace and civic centre in Roman towns

Forum Boarium (*for*-um boh-*are*-ee-um)

famous cattle market in Rome near the Tiber and the round Temple of Hercules

fulcrum (*full*-krum)

curved part at the head of a couch (usually a dining couch)

funalis (foo-*nah*-liss)

one of the horses which was harnessed to the chariot to the left or right of the yoked pair by traces or 'funes'

genius (*jeen*-yuss)

Latin for guardian spirit, usually of the home but also of a person

gladiator

man trained to fight other men in the arena, sometimes to the death

gustatio (goo-*stat*-yo)

first course or 'starter' of a Roman banquet

Hercules (*her*-kyoo-leez)

    very popular Roman demi-god, the equivalent of Greek Herakles

herm

    squared pillar with a sculpted head (often of Hermes) and male private parts, to avert bad luck

hippodrome (*hip*-oh-drome)

    'racecourse'; from the Greek words *hippos* 'horse' and *dromos* 'run'

hortatores (hor-ta-*tore*-raze)

    Latin for 'encouragers'; they sometimes rode on horse-back to encourage their team

impluvium (im-*ploo*-vee-um)

    rectangular rainwater pool under a skylight (compluvium) in the atrium

Incitatus (inky-*ta*-tuss)

    famous race-horse belonging to the Emperor Caligula; he had his own marble stall at the Stables of the Greens and Caligula considered making him consul

Italia (it-*al*-ya)

    the Latin word for Italy

iugales (yoo-*gal*-laze)

    the two central horses of a chariot team, so-called because they ran beneath the 'iugum' or yoke

Janus (*jan*-uss)

    Roman god of doorways and beginnings

Judea (joo-*dee*-uh)

    ancient province of the Roman Empire; part of modern Israel

Juno (*joo*-no)

    queen of the Roman gods and wife of the god Jupiter

Jupiter (*joo*-pit-er)

    king of the Roman gods, husband of Juno and brother of Pluto and Neptune

Kalends (*kal*-ends)

    the first day of any month in the Roman calendar

kohl (*coal*)

    dark powder used to darken eyelids or outline eyes

lararium (lar-*ar*-ee-um)

    household shrine, often a chest with a miniature temple on top, sometimes a niche

Lares (*lah*-raze)

    household gods

linea alba (*lin*-ee-uh *al*-buh)

    white line chalked across the ancient Roman racetrack at the beginning of the euripus; no chariot was allowed to break for position until it crossed this line

Ludi Romani (*loo*-dee ro-*mah*-nee)

    games (especially chariot races) in honour of Jupiter, held from 5th-19th September

lynchpin

    vital pin passed through the axle-end of a vehicle to keep the wheel in place

mappa (*map*-uh)

    napkin-like cloth dropped by magistrate to mark the beginning of a race

mecastor! (mee-*kas*-tore)

    exclamation based on the name Castor, suitable for a Roman lady to use; probably rather old-fashioned by the time this story takes place

Medusa (m-*dyoo*-suh)

    mythical female monster with a face so ugly she turned

men to stone; when her head was cut off, the winged horse Pegasus sprang from her neck

meta (*met*-uh)

turning point at each end of a racecourse; in the Circus Maximus, each meta was marked by three tall bronze cones, grouped together on semi-circular platforms

miliarius (mill-ee-*are*-ee-uss)

charioteer who has won over a thousand (*mille*) races

Minerva (min-*erv*-uh)

Roman equivalent of Athena, the Greek goddess of wisdom, war, philosophy and women's arts

moratores (more-ah-*tore*-raze)

Latin for 'delayers'; they probably calmed the horses in the starting gates

Murcia (*murce*-ya)

also known as Venus Murcia; this ancient goddess had a shrine with a myrtle bush on the actual racetrack of the Circus, near the stands at the curved end

naufragium (now-*frog*-ee-um)

Latin for 'shipwreck'; what the crowd cried out when one or more chariots crashed

Neapolis (nee-*ap*-o-liss)

major city of Campania (modern Naples)

Neptune (*nep*-tyoon)

god of the sea and of horses; his Greek equivalent is Poseidon

Nero (*near*-oh)

Emperor who ruled Rome from AD 54–69

Nomentum (no-*men*-tum)

region of the Sabines, northeast of Rome; NB: there is no evidence that the Greens had a stud farm here

Nones (nonz)

Seventh day of March, May, July, October; fifth day of the others, including September

Oenomaeus (ee-no-*may*-uss)

Greek king who rigged a chariot race against suitors for the hand of his daughter

ohe! (*oh*-hay)

Latin exclamation meaning 'Whoa!' or 'Stop!'

Ostia (*oss*-tee-uh)

port about 16 miles southwest of Rome; Ostia is Flavia's home town

Ovid (*ov*-id)

Publius Ovidius Naso (43 BC–AD 17); Roman poet whose works include love poetry as well as the less well-known *Fasti*

palaestra (puh-*lice*-tra)

exercise area of public baths, usually a sandy courtyard open to the sky

palla (*pal*-uh)

a woman's cloak, could also be wrapped round the waist or worn over the head

papyrus (puh-*pie*-russ)

papery material made of pounded Egyptian reeds, used as writing paper and also for parasols and fans

patina (pa-*teen*-uh)

Latin for 'dish' or 'pan': a kind of flan with eggs, either savoury or sweet

Pelops (*pee*-lops)

Greek who bribed a groom to replace the bronze linchpin in his opponent's chariot with a wax one; it melted with friction and Oenomaeus was thrown and killed

Penates (pen-*ah*-taze)
> household gods, especially of the larder, where food is kept

peristyle (*perry*-style)
> a columned walkway around an inner garden or courtyard

plebeian (pleb-*ee*-un)
> from Latin 'plebs'; one of the common people or 'lower classes', as opposed to those of the equestrian and patrician class

Pollux (*pol*-luks)
> one of the famous twins of Greek mythology (Castor being the other)

pompa (*pom*-puh)
> procession; on the first and last day of a festival celebrated with chariot races, there would be a procession around the track of the emperor, dignitaries, faction members, musicians, dancers, entertainers and statues of the gods

Pons Fabricius (ponz fab-*rick*-ee-uss)
> ancient bridge in Rome leading to the Tiber Island, you can still see its four-faced herms

Pontifex Maximus (*pon*-tee-fecks *mack*-sim-uss)
> Latin for 'highest priest'; this was often the emperor, as in this story

portico (*por*-tik-oh)
> roof supported by columns, often attached as a porch to a building or surrounding a garden

posca (*poss*-kuh)
> well-watered vinegar; a non-alcoholic drink particularly favoured by soldiers on duty

Praetorian Guard (pry-*tor*-ee-an gard)

special soldiers chosen to guard the Emperor

prasini (pra-*see*-nee)

Latin for 'Greens', i.e. the Green Faction

probatio equorum (pro-*bah*-tee-oh eh-*kwor*-um)

literally: 'testing of horses'; on the day before the races horses would be checked for fitness by a veterinarian and perhaps given trial runs in the hippodrome

pulvinar (*puhl*-vin-ar)

large covered box on the Palatine side of the Circus Maximus, statues of the gods 'watched' the chariot races from here

Pythia (*pith*-ee-uh)

priestess who uttered the oracular responses of Apollo at Delphi

quadriga (*kwad*-rig-uh)

a chariot pulled by four horses, the central two yoked, the outer two on traces

russati (roo-*sah*-tee)

Latin for 'Reds', i.e. the Red Faction

salvete! (sal-*vay*-tay)

'hello' to more than one person ('salve' is 'hello' to one person)

Samaritan (sa-*mare*-it-an)

native of Samaria, a region of Israel; Samaritans were not always accepted by the strictly observant Jews of Jerusalem

Scorpus (*skorp*-uss)

famous charioteer of the late first century AD who won over 2,000 races and who died aged 27, probably as a result of a racing accident

scroll (skrole)

papyrus or parchment 'book', unrolled from side to side as it was read

Scythian (*sith*-ee-un)

native of Scythia, a region north of the Black Sea; in ancient times it was famous for its nomadic tribes of pony-riding barbarians

sedan-chair

mode of conveyance carried by strong men or slaves, like a litter, but the rider sits instead of reclining

selah lanu et hovoteynu (s'-*lach*-lah-noo et-ho-vo-*tane*-oo)

Hebrew: 'Forgive us our debts . . .'

sesterces (sess-*tur*-seez)

more than one *sestertius*, a brass coin; about a day's wage for a labourer

sparsores (spar-*sore*-raze)

boys who sprinkled horses to refresh them and the track to keep the dust down

spina (*spee*-nah)

Latin for 'spine'; one of the words used to describe the euripus or central barrier of a racecourse

strigil (*strij*-ill)

blunt-edged, curved tool for scraping off dead skin, oil and dirt at the baths; they were used for horses as well as people

stylus (*stile*-us)

metal, wood or ivory tool for writing on wax tablets

Surrentum (sir-*wren*-tum)

modern Sorrento, a pretty harbour town on the Bay of Naples south of Vesuvius

synthesis (sinth-ess-is)

    garment worn by men at dinner parties, perhaps a long, unbelted tunic with a short mantle of matching colour

tablinum (tab-*leen*-um)

    room in wealthier Roman houses used as the master's study or office, often looking out onto the atrium or inner garden, or both

tiro (*teer*-oh)

    novice charioteer, gladiator or soldier

Titus (*tie*-tuss)

    Titus Flavius Vespasianus, 40 year old son of Vespasian, has been Emperor of Rome for just over a year when this story takes place

toga praetexta (*toe*-ga pry-*tecks*-ta)

    purple-edged blanket-like outer garment, worn by boys and senators, (most men over 16 wore the plain white toga virilis)

triclinium (trik-*lin*-ee-um)

    ancient Roman dining room, usually with three couches to recline on

Trigarium (trig-ar-ee-um)

    an open space in Rome where horses were exercised, probably in the north-west part of the Campus Martius, near the bank of the river Tiber

tunic (*tew*-nic)

    piece of clothing like a big T-shirt; children often wore a long-sleeved one

veneti (*ven*-eh-tee)

    Latin for 'Blues', i.e. the Blue Faction

Vesta (*vest*-uh)
> goddess of the hearth; remains of her temple in Rome can still be seen today

vigiles (*vig*-ill-aze)
> Roman policemen/firemen; the word means 'watchmen'

wax tablet
> wax-coated rectangular piece of wood used for making notes

LAST SCROLL

Chariot races in ancient Rome were even more popular than gladiatorial combats. Everybody had an opinion about the races and everybody supported one of the four factions. Many charioteers were as popular as movie stars are today, and as rich. One such charioteer was Flavius Scorpus. In this story I have made him autistic, a condition which was unidentified in the Roman world. I have also made him Greek, but we don't really know where he came from. What we do know is that he won 2,048 races before his death aged 27 around AD 95. This information comes from the Roman poet Martial, who wrote several epigrams mentioning Scorpus and also two elegies. Here is one of the elegies:

> *I was Scorpus, young star of the noisy circus and darling of Rome. Envious Death took me too soon: counting the number of my victories, he thought I was old!*
>
> *Martial X.53*

Today, the Circus Maximus is a long grassy field in the centre of Rome. In ancient times it was a monumental building around a long racecourse, able to seat

241

nearly a quarter of a million people and provide them with food, water, latrines and souvenirs. Some souvenirs which have survived until today are moulded blown-glass 'chariot beakers'. A perfectly-preserved sea-greeen beaker from Colchester of Roman Britain shows the monuments of the spina of the Circus Maximus with four chariots racing round it. The four characters are named Olympus, Antiloctius, Cresces and Hierax.

Today you can still see one of the barrier monuments – a lofty obelisk erected by Augustus – in the Piazza del Popolo in Rome.

Most of us get our idea of Roman chariot racing from the 1959 Oscar-winning film *Ben-Hur*. The famous chariot-race is one of the most exciting action scenes in cinema history, but there are some inaccuracies: the chariots were not big and heavy but small and very light; the charioteers wrapped the reins around their waists and always wore leather helmets; the number of chariots in any race was a multiple of four; and seven laps were run, not ten. During the filming of the earlier, 1925 silent version of *Ben-Hur*, there was a terrible pile-up in which men and horses really died. This gives the best idea of what a Roman chariot race would have been like, if you can bear to watch!